THIRTEEN STEPS
TOWARDS THE FATE
OF ERIKA KLAUS

a novel
by Kazat Akmatov

Hertfordshire Press
London 2013

Published in United Kindom
Hertforfshire Press © 2013
(Imprint of Silk Road Media)

Suite 125, 43 Bedford Street
Covent Garden, London
WC2 9HA United Kingdom
www.hertfordshirepress.com

Design & Typeset by Aleksandra Vlasova
Illustrations by Varvara Perekrest
Translated: Elizabeth Adams
Edited: Laura Hamilton

British Library Catalogue in Publication Data
A catalogue record for this book is available from the British Library
Library of Congress in Publication Data
A catalogue record for this book has been requested

ISBN 978-0957480766

Contents

About the author

Kazat Akmatov was born at the beginning of the World War II, in Bosteri in the Kyrgyz Republic of the Soviet Union. Both his own father and his adoptive father perished and hence, locals named the young orphan *Kazat*, meaning *war* or *fight*. His talent as a narrator emerged early and when he was between ten and twelve, he was punished at school for detaining his classmates with his stories. At fifteen he was commissioned to write a play for his school. *The Rich Landowner and the Day Labourers* was applauded, although its high standard led parents to suspect that it had been plagiarized from work by Soviet writers on class struggle.

While studying journalism, Akmatov confined his poetry to notebooks, believing that serious subject matter was better presented in prose. Having already worked for the Komsomol (the youth division of the All-Union Communist party) and served as an officer in the Soviet army, he was committed to a career as a writer after finishing University. Instead, he was ordered to join the army by the USSR's Minister of Defense, purportedly to strengthen the ranks. KGB spies had long suspected him of being a nationalist and "immature" communist and the Party organization of the military part of the "Guards" within the Central Asian Military District raised the exclusion of Lieutenant Akmatov from the Communist Party. He was recognized as guilty for asking: "How much time does it take to declassify documents in the Soviet Union, in accordance with the law?"

As a consequence, his first novel *Two Strings of Life* was not published until 1972. Successful on many levels, it entered the Party's stream of criticism against corrupt officials from the Soviet economic organs. Akmatov was awarded the Nikolai Ostrovsky Prize: the most prestigious accolade for young writers of the USSR. The next stage in Akmatov's oeuvre, characterized by novels *Earth*

Time and *Years around the Sun* as well as the play, *Night of Divorce*, proved life-changing. All three works were imbued with the author's compassion for the tragic fate of Kyrgyz people. The media however, submissive to taunts by the Communist Party, printed a series of derogatory articles. Examined by the Central Committee of the Communist Party, *Earth Time* was declared "anti-Russian" and *Years around the Sun,* "anti-Soviet". *Night of Divorce* was pronounced to be "anti-Party", and the Ministry of Culture closed the play and even set alight the props. The author felt attacked from all sides: he was fired from his job in journalism; his books were withdrawn from sale, and the Party ensured that he received none of the high awards and prizes which he had won. No-one would publish Kazat Akmatov.

In retaliation, Akmatov publicly announced his withdrawal from the Communist Party and began to organize the Democratic Movement of Kyrgyzstan. This movement which demanded the separation of Kyrgyzstan from the Soviet Union, the elimination of the Communist Party in Kyrgyzstan and the declaration of independence for Kyrgyzstan, came to fruition in 1991.

After five years in politics as a Member of Parliament, Akmatov returned to writing and much of his work is now published in many languages. His novel *Arhat*, available in five languages, has won several international prizes and the State Prize of Kyrgyzstan.

Thirteen Steps towards the Fate of Erika Klaus has been well acclaimed. Based on a true incident, it follows the tragic fate of an extraordinary and naïve young Norwegian woman, who arrives in Kyrgyzstan as a Peace Corps volunteer. Set in a remote outpost, where a fascist hide-out has emerged from the ruins of the former Soviet Union, this work explores the daily brutality faced by both Klaus and as significantly, the Kyrgyz people around her .

A writer rather than a politician, Akmatov nevertheless, continues to raise awareness of the oppression of basic human rights throughout Asia and following his description of the brutal regime in Chet, his new novel *Shahidka* highlights the fate of the Chechen nation and its eternal fight for freedom through a love story between a young Chechen man and a young Russian woman.

All evil is perpetrated under the flag of truth and justice.
— Kazat Akmatov

THE FIRST STEP: ON KYRGYZ SOIL

"Something's happening on the sun." The half-formed thought came to Erika while she was still asleep, like an intuition. It was, in fact, a faint sign of vitamin D deficiency. It was a feeling the girl recognized. She experienced it from time to time, especially on days when she had a terrible time waking up in the morning. It was a painful sensation that gnawed at her heart, painful enough to force her awake. Her thoughts and her headstrong personality awoke with her.

"My God: I'm in Bishkek!" Erika realized as she crawled out of bed. "This place is wonderful," She smiled weakly. Even through the closed curtains she could feel the midday sun of Central Asia, white-hot in the July sky.

"I've dreamt about this my whole life! And here is my sun!"

No local would ever subject the naked eye to a study of the hottest point in the sky. They preferred to sit somewhere cool, hiding away from the sun's powerful radiation, avoiding heatstroke. Only Erika and others like her were crazy enough to test their eyes against the sun. She did it because she was born and raised in the far north of Europe, further than misty Albion, in the Kingdom of Norway. This was her second trip to the southern climate she loved, and every corner of her mind and fibre of her body was focused on the sun and nothing but the sun.

Erika opened the window and stuck her head out, craning her neck to look at the sun soaring in the sky high above the roof of the high-rise apartment building where her friend Aigul lived.

"And they say the sun shines the same everywhere," Erika thought ironically. "Back in Scandinavia it never shines like it does here. That must simply be a fact of our solar system, and there's not a thing we can do about it. I'm glad Aigul got me away from the wet and cold. Although who knows, maybe I didn't do the right thing to follow her here, solely on the basis of her intriguing stories. But there's an interesting saying here: 'If you never take risks you'll never drink champagne.' I'll take things as they come and I won't go back on my plans. I just hope people here aren't as aggressive as my parents think. Everything else will take care of itself. As long as I'm careful and keep my eyes open."

As far back as she could remember, Erika had known her own body as well as her parents had. Later, when she grew up and began learning about science, she gleaned more information about the rickets she had suffered during her sun-deprived childhood in the overcast north. She came to know more about the disease than her parents, and this was often the cause of arguments between them.

Erika's parents, a theologian and historian, had a nostalgic view of the time of their ancient ancestors, the Vikings, who worshipped that king of the gods, Odin. The sun meant everything to the sea-faring Vikings. It was their compass and a source of warmth; it gave them hope of victory over their enemies and they worshipped it, spinning many tales, legends, sayings and songs about the sun. Steeped in its ancient lore ,Erika's outwardly modern parents instructed her to worship the sun instead of wasting her time on scientific books and journals.

Eventually, when Erika was thoroughly tired of arguing with them, she declared:"Fine. I'll make the sun my talisman. Maybe I'll even follow it to the edge of the earth where it rises early in the morning."

Her parents made nothing of this because they didn't really understand what she meant.

When she graduated from university with a degree in English and a teacher's certificate and abruptly announced to her parents that she was going to a place called Kyrgyzia to volunteer with the Peace Corps, her mother and father became hysterical.

To calm them, she told them about her friends who had already volunteered in far-away Asian countries. She also told them that she had met a Kyrgyz girl at the university in Oslo, and that the girl had invited her to Bishkek. Her parents refused to accept a word she said.

Then, in a tone that put an end to all discussion, Erika cut them off, "You found your own paths in life without anyone giving you advice or attacking your decisions. So now let me find my own way!"

*∗∗

Once she had arrived in Bishkek after spending over ten hours napping uncomfortably in the plane, Erika realized that she had been much too hard on her parents.

"But what's done is done," she told herself. "I can't look back. And at least I've finally found the real sun I always dreamed of. Something must be happening on the surface of the sun today: A burst of solar energy. I suppose it's sending off long strings of flares. I can feel them all over. The solar wind is affecting Earth's magnetic field. That's what causes the sharp pains I feel in my chest sometimes and on the sores on my legs that won't heal." These were her thoughts as she stood in the middle of a street bazaar where a sea of melons was giving off the heady scent of summertime in the mountains and plains. The melons were arranged in neat rows on the ground, with their bases up and their tails down so that customers could see at a glance which of them were "girls" and which were "boys." Erika noticed that people were buying more "girls" than "boys". That made her laugh. So did the fact that to her eyes, all the Asian faces looked the same. She stood there for almost half an hour, greedily inhaling the scent of the melons, the scent of the true southern sun, whilst trying to distinguish differences in the round faces with narrow eyes that shuffled around the melons. She wasn't very good at it.

"I swear they all look alike," she finally admitted to herself. Then she noticed how few European faces there were of the kind she was used to, with large, friendly blue eyes.

The aroma of the melons seeped into Erika's whole body through millions of capillaries, invigorating her blood and, of course, elevating her soul.

A Speck Of Fresh Earth

In *Chet,*[1] Colonel Bronza took his favorite fighting dog Cerberus for their usual walk up a nearby mountain path, between eleven o'clock and one. Colonal Bronza was wearing nothing but red shorts and had a pair of powerful binoculars slung over one shoulder. The head of the border post, called *Kagan*[2] by the local Kyrgyz, had not yet decided what kind of mood he was in.

---

1 Chet – A remote village settlement. The word "chet" means "edge," which was the name given to the Soviet border post established there in the 1930s and closed in the late 1990s after the fall of the Soviet Union.
2 Kagan – (Kyrgyz) Leader.

He did not want to waste the two hours of sunshine on a mere walk, so while he was waiting for important ideas about possible career manoeuvres to come to into his head, he studied the path. He wanted to see if the soldiers had dropped any debris from the fresh earth they had dug the night before.

The border post's dogs were locked in their enclosure. When they caught wind of Cerberus walking by, they gave him a friendly bark. It was a sign of dog envy on their part. In addition to his extra daily walks with the master, Cerberus had his own special cage and ate his meals alone under Bronza's loving eye. Because of this, Cerberus, who was extremely playful and happy at this time of day, paid absolutely no attention to the noise his brothers were raising. He kept pulling ahead with his large, stately body, forcing his master to yank frequently at the leash in his fist.

Despite that distraction, the colonel managed to examine every inch of the dry, gray path in hope of finding even one speck of fresh earth. So far he hadn't found any, and no new ideas had come into his head.

When he reached the end of the path, Colonel Bronza carefully inspected the darkening base of the deep ravine where his soldiers had been directed to deposit the earth which they had brought up in bags before covering it meticulously with fresh branches. There were no signs of fresh earth, so Bronza was pleased. But he saw that the ravine was almost half-full. That worried him: would all of the earth dug out from his future underground bunker fit in the ravine? What if it didn't? Where could they find a similar natural ravine? That was important. There must be no signs whatsoever of the large, secret project he had been commanding for almost a year. If anyone discovered the tiniest indication, it would be the end of Bronza, the project's architect and contractor. God willing, as early as next year the bunker would become the key element of an enormous system which the head of the border post had already mapped out in his mind.

"It may not be the same as the bunkers built by powerful Hitler or great Stalin," he thought to himself ecstatically, "but it will be Bronza's bunker. Be sure of that! The bunker of tomorrow is moving full steam ahead today. I can already see my officers and soldiers getting fat. Those bastards," he thought to himself, "have gone behind my back and opened numbered accounts in a bunch of foreign banks so they can stuff their wallets on the quiet. Each one of them has more than one wife, and they're feeding mouths back in Russia pretty well. And it's all thanks to me. Thanks to my brain. Thanks to my blood and sweat. Hitler couldn't have done it, could he? Or Stalin? Or that what's-his-name, Mussolini? What did they ever give their freeloaders but three-day marauding trips? Nothing! But I give them all they want in pure, green paper! And the aborigines? They lick my ass, every last one of them, young and old, women and men. Every last one of the women is willing to lie under me and stack their bastards up in a pile, all because I feed them! Bread buys everything!

"God willing, I'll finish my bunker and invite the presidents of friendly nations here to take a look at how they ought to feed their people. They'll come into my main hall and see my decree: 'Whoever is not with me is my enemy!' and then they can draw their own conclusions. If anyone doesn't like it, there's the road!"

Just then, out of the corner of his eye, the colonel noticed the far-off shadow of some birds flying above the high cliff opposite to where he stood. He hurriedly raised his binoculars to his eyes. It was a small flock of golden eagles, including young birds that had been born that year. The colonel was always delighted to see golden eagles. His left hand held the binoculars while his right hand found his pocket flask. He took a quick swallow of Scotch whiskey. The blood pounded merrily in his temples. He took another swallow and then capped the flask and put it back. Bronza lay back on the grass with his bare chest exposed to the midday sun, already beginning to disappear behind the cliffs where the golden eagles soared.

"Wonderful!" the colonel exclaimed aloud. "That's just beautiful! The eagles are the only birds that fly over the peaks. Kings of the blue sky! God made them simply magnificent!"

After the eagles and their young spiraled had higher and higher in the sky and disappeared out of range of his binoculars, the colonel stood and looked toward Chet. As usual, the locals were lying outside their homes or sitting on benches with their shirts off to take advantage of the two hours of sunshine. The Kyrgyz of Chet call themselves sun worshipers.

The first time Bronza heard that, he gave a good laugh. "But they're god-damn Muslims! Don't they know what god they're supposed to pray to? When the party committee sent me here from Moscow to head the border post, they told me to study the aborigines' habits and customs. Now I know them like the back of my hand. They're a clever people, though," he reflected. "But they drink too much and don't bathe enough. That's why they all stink. And the bastards don't like to work. All they want is to get their *soms*[3] out of me. I say let them work for me. The chump change they get from me doesn't amount to much. And they provide local cover for my Post. As long as I feed them and their children, that's a gag on the Kyrgyz government. I knew what I was doing when I hung their flag next to the Russian flag at the Post. If I have to, I'll re-name the Post in honour of some old *basmach*[4] and hang a portrait of whoever the president is in my waiting room. They'll die and go to heaven!

"But I'm siding with Russia for now. Nobody here knows that Moscow demobilized my unit. You've got to give it to Moscow. They demobilized their own faithful border unit and then forgot all about it. They've got plenty of units like mine all around the world. That's more than they can count, and definitely more than they want to pay to move.

"What if my soldiers and officers make their way back home and go knocking on doors like a bunch of gypsies? Do you think the big bureaucrats will notice them? Do think they care about their families living in poverty, or about their lack of a future in the army? Not a chance. The new Mother Russia tossed out all of its patriots. Most of them are on the streets. I see their pathetic faces on the television every day.

"It's a disgrace, and I won't stand for it. I'll stay right here in these Kyrgyz mountains and keep all my men with me. The main thing is to keep them from finding out about the demobilization and running home. I need to keep all my men here for now. I'll be expanding in the future!"

While the colonel made his way down to the border post, interspersing his brave, animated thoughts with his usual thick Russian profanity, he was suddenly struck by fear. The fear came from the fact that the sun was de-scending rapidly behind the cliffs. All around him darkness descended over the Chet gorge, and the Chet River turned black in an instant. At moments like

3 Som – *Kyrgyz national currency*
4 Basmach – *A counter- revolutionary*

this it seemed to the colonel that time was flying away from him like an arrow beyond his control.

"They're taking too long!" he thought, grinding his teeth and thinking about the building of his bunker. "Those goddamn soldiers are taking their sweet time."

Here his angry eyes accidentally noticed a few specks of fresh red earth on the path that had been flattened by boots.

"Assholes!" the colonel yelled.

He took several more swallows of whiskey from his flask and walked decisively down to the border post. Shortly afterwards, his "turds" were sent down to the horses' winter stable where the soldiers who had dragged bags of earth to the ravine the night before were locked up. Then the kicking began, administered by three "turds" to one soldier.

It had been the colonel's idea to call them "turds". There weren't many of them, just a few soldiers who were the dregs of his unit; drug addicts, alcoholics and others who were just too stupid to do anything. When they were younger, they had been beaten up, as had Bronza, by other kids their age, tormented for being physically and mentally weak. In later life Bronza was lucky. After being drafted, he was sent to a school for sergeants and then to the border service. When, through an irony of fate, he found himself in the powerful position of head of the border post, he was overcome by a desire for revenge against those stronger than himself and, at the same time, by that most primitive of male cravings, the desire for power over others.

Bronza noticed that whenever he punished soldiers, the turds would rush to help him beat the men to a pulp. They seemed to want to ingratiate themselves with the boss while proving their importance at the Post. They also seemed to enjoy demonstrating their power over the men being punished. They could beat them as much as they wanted and never answer for it.

The colonel liked the turds' animal behavior. He realized that if he beat up the soldiers every time they got in trouble, it would cause dangerous levels of animosity to accumulate among the men. It would be better to use the angry bastards at the bottom of the barrel for this necessary but ignoble job. It wouldn't hurt to have them on board. After all, even though he enforced tyrannical discipline, the colonel always felt that there wasn't enough discipline and order at the post.

THE SECOND STEP: HEADING FOR THE SUN

Erika got into the shabby yellow Moskvich with a heavy heart. When the driver got out of the car and walked over to take her things to put them in the boot, her first thought had been that he had a very unpleasant face and scary eyes. She had been looking forward to meeting him all morning and had prepared herself for a pleasant, interesting encounter. She had been told that she would have to ride with this man for five or six hours along empty mountain roads, so she went out of her way to prime herself for being friendly to him. But there is no forcing the heart: Sometimes we just don't like the look of people.

The driver was experiencing almost the same disappointment. When he went to the Education Ministry warehouse to load textbooks for the school in Chet, he heard that he would have to stop by the Peace Corps office and pick up a young foreign teacher.

"And take her all the way to Chet?" he asked, narrowing his eyes and looking annoyed at the additional responsibility.

In his heart, though, he felt a rustling curiosity. "I bet she's pretty. Of course she is: she's young and she's a foreigner." But when he saw her come out of the Peace Corps building accompanied by two other women, he immediately saw that she was no beauty. Up close, his first impression was confirmed when the pale young woman who looked to be about twenty, reached out and shook his hand. A too-pale face marked by signs of depression, surrounded by pale blond hair, blond eyelashes and eyebrows and two large front teeth that jutted out ever so slightly: those were the extent of her charms. Her smile was obviously forced, and her eyes looked afraid and distrusting. It was easy to see that she didn't want to get into the ramshackle car.

"Don't worry, Erika," said Aigul. "He is my relative. He's reliable. Get in the car and go with him. If anything goes wrong, call my mobile. I'll be in touch with you the whole way."

"It's okay. We've written down his license plate number!" joked the woman from the Peace Corps, and with that, the Moskvich lurched away from the kerb, rattling loudly in protest of the heavy load.

The two rode along in silence. Neither of them liked the other. They gave no indication of the fact, but the silence made them feel uncomfortable. It especially irked Erika, since she was not used to keeping her opinions about anything or anyone to herself. After all, she was a member of the Emo Club in Oslo, and it went against the club's rules. Freedom of thought and speech, the freedom to express all your natural feelings openly, aloud and without hiding anything ; these were the standards by which the freedom- loving Emos measured their behavior.

Erika had spent many of her young adult years at the club and was in complete agreement with its principles. The only true, natural path to prosperity and internal harmony was to live on Earth the way human nature intended. In the stagnant, trivial society of Norway, this youthful philosophy of the probing heart mainly attracted students of a romantic bent who wore bright pink and brown clothes to stand out from the bleak crowds. All of them were searching for the meaning of life, and Erika was especially zealous in this regard.

Erika began to get annoyed with the driver because she thought he was pretending to be more focused on his driving than he actually was.

"What's the big deal?" she wondered. "The car does all the work. All he has to do is sit there and steer." She began to think of a way to tell him this.

As if on cue, the Moskvich heaved to one side and began bumping over some rocks in the road, making it almost impossible to steer. The driver threw all his weight against the wheel, gripping it with both hands as if he were fighting a wild animal. Steep, dark cliffs towered over the road and at times they resembled terrible giants moving along in great leaps.

Overcome with sudden terror, Erika gripped her seat with both hands. "Are the cliffs falling towards us?" she cried. Her voice was desperate.

The grim driver laughed for the first time. "The cliffs aren't falling, but sometimes rocks slide off them." His voice bounced with the car.

"What does 'slide' mean?"

"Rocks fall off the cliffs and land here on the road."

"Oh my God! Are many people killed?"

"One in a thousand."

"One in a thousand? Is that much?"

"Of course not. It isn't much at all."

"God! How can you do this?"

Erika retreated into herself for a while. Then she roused herself and asked, "Are you afraid of the rocks?"

"Of course everyone's afraid."

"I've read many tourist guides. All promote Kyrgyzstan as a very good country, with lots of sunshine. I love the sun. That's why I came. I didn't know that Kyrgyzstan had rocks that fall on people."

The driver laughed again. "Rocks don't fall on people every day. Sometimes earthquakes cause the rocks to slide. But it doesn't happen all the time."

Erika gave him a skeptical look before asking the question that had been bothering her for the whole trip. "Why haven't you told me your name?"

"I completely forgot. My name is Sovietbek. This damn road doesn't leave me much time to talk..." He offered her his hand.

"Say your name again, please." Erika asked as she shook his hand.

"Sovietbek."

"That's a good name."

"It's a stupid name."

"Why?" Erika's eyes grew round.

"The Kyrgyz are too easy to push around. Back in Soviet times they named all their kids after Soviet stuff, like we didn't have any better names of our own. You can meet people with ridiculous names like Combine and Tractor. There's not another country in the world where people act like that."

"You don't like your people?"

"Why should I like them? They make too many stupid mistakes."

"He isn't interested in my name at all", Erika thought in annoyance. Her woman's pride was injured.

No sooner had she turned her face to the window than Sovietbek asked, "So what's your name?"

Erika didn't want to answer him, but she had no choice. "Erika," she said dryly.

Sovietbek became animated. "Wow! What a wonderful name. When I was in the army I had a penpal, this girl from Kazan. Her name was Erika, too. She was a Tatar."

"How interesting", Erika thought sarcastically. Aloud, she merely asked, "Do we have much further to go? I'm very tired."

The Moskvich began to bounce over more potholes preventing the driver from talking.

When the bumping lessened, Sovietbek, who was feeling a pang of pity in his heart, turned and asked, "Who told you to go to Chet? I'd like to know."

"I made my own choice."

"I bet you didn't know where Chet was, did you?"

"I read that there are many sun worshippers in Chet. I loved that!"

For a long time, Sovietbek said nothing and pretended to be engaged with the road again. Meanwhile, the mountain pass they were traveling through grew swiftly dark. The silhouettes of the few houses they passed were cloaked in shadows. This frightened Erika.

"It got dark very fast," she said, making a helpless gesture with her hands. She didn't know which way to turn her head. They were surrounded in darkness. Erika got no response. All she could see was the driver's fine, strong teeth in the corner of his smile. Now his unattractive face seemed downright scary, and his teeth were like fangs.

The silence continued for a while.

Suddenly the driver broke in with a question. "So you love sun worshippers?"

"I'm one, too." Erika said. She did not turn to face him. Her voice sounded strained.

The pitch black outside the car windows forced Erika to watch the road ahead, which was illuminated by the headlights, and to look at the few objects close to her, inside the car. The girl took note of the way the driver's hands gripped the wheel. They were rough. The skin on his joints was cracked, and his fingers and palms were yellow on the bottom and dark red on top. Out of the corner of her eye, Erika noticed that Sovietbek's first finger was short, as if part of it had been lopped off.

"That's obviously a sign of aggression and a bad temper", Erika decided. She tried not to look at the driver anymore.

Instead, she distracted herself by remembering her friends in Oslo. All of a sudden she began to hear her mother's reprimanding voice: "It's all because of that ridiculous Emo club of yours. They're the ones who taught you to do whatever you want and all sorts of other nonsense. How can you dance around with other girls in front of everyone and yell whatever comes into your head? You ought to be ashamed of yourself! And then you come home and disrespect your parents just because we won't go along with your stupidity! It's all my fault. I'm the one who let you run wild. I'm the one who convinced your father to open a bank account for you. Now your father and I are paying for our mistakes. Our daughter is a wild egotist who takes a job who knows where without even coming to us for advice first. I hope those barbarians tear you to pieces. Or maybe the bearded terrorists will cut your head off. That'll teach you to ignore your mother."

"But you raised me to be a sun worshipper. Remember how you used to tell me that when I was a baby I would pull away from your breast and scream and cry until you carried me outside to look at the sun? I don't know how many times you've told me that story."

"So what? The sun is no reason to make an utter fool of yourself."

"Lots of other students have volunteered there before and no one ever got their head cut off."

"Well when they do cut it off, it'll be too late."

Erika dismissed her with the same categorical pronouncement she had used before. "Know what, Mum? You found your way in life on your own. Now let me find mine!"

Her mother and father fell silent. Erika was proud. She had finally beaten down her tired, grey-haired parents.

THE THIRD STEP – A MORNING WITH NO SUN

It was late when Erika arrived at Chet, and she spent the night at the house of the Curriculum Director of the school that had opened nine years ago. In the morning she walked out into the unfamiliar yard. Her steps were tentative when she walked, as if she were sliding over ice. Her eyes, surprised and captivated, were focused on one little spot of life; a tiny, stray dog which was barking hysterically. The dog had been hastily tied to a bush near the house, but the rope that was supposed to hold it was so thin and worn that the school's curriculum director, whose name was Samara Orunbayev, feared for Erika's safety and pushed her into her house.

"When you come back out she won't bark at you anymore," Samara Orunbayeva assured her.

"I knew immediately that dog was smart," Erika replied with a radiant smile as she walked into the living room.

Her eyes grew even wider when she saw the collection of animal skins spread out on the floor and hanging on the walls. The skins were all colours and sizes, each with four paws and a head. They belonged to many different animals, none of which Erika recognized.

"The Green Party in Oslo would file a lawsuit against anyone who had even one of these skins", she was thinking, but she asked her hostess something completely different. "Did your husband or son kill all those?"

"We inherited them all from our grandfathers," Samara Orunbayeva said with a laugh. She saw that her guest was imagining how the animals had been killed and skinned, so she added an explanation. "We cover the floor and walls with them to keep the room warm. You'll be warm all winter."

"But isn't it very sunny here? It gets hot doesn't it?"

"We almost never see the sun. In the summer it shines for just two hours a day. In the winter it all but disappears. But we know the sun loves us."

"Why?" Erika cried. Her face was pale. "I came for sun. In the ads they say that Kyrgyzstan has a lot of sunshine." She gestured helplessly with her hands again.

"That's true, but we don't get much here in Chet. That's why we catch all the rays we can in the summer to feed our bodies before the winter."

"What do you mean 'feed?' "

"You'll understand in time. You'll see for yourself. You'll be just fine."

"If there's no sunshine, I'll leave. Okay?" Erika asked waveringly.

"It's true, sweetheart, you didn't come at the best time. Everything is different here. And then there's Kagan. I mean the head of the border post. He feeds us with one hand and cuts us down with the other. For now at least. I don't know what will happen in the future, but that's how it is for now. But as far as you're concerned, all you have to do is teach our children English. Don't think about anything else. It will be better that way. When the border guards ask you about anything, always speak and write the truth. There's no other way to save yourself. That's what we do. We don't have any way out. All of us here in Chet live on the truth. The truth feeds us and it gives us life! Our Kagan has a saying. It's not the same as what Dostoyevsky said, but it's close: "Truth saves the world!" I think it sounds pretty good."

"I love the truth, too. Only the truth." Erika answered.

She looked at Samara Orunbayeva for a long time with disappointed eyes. Her mouth opened on its own, revealing her two large front teeth. Her lips trembled. She was either about to burst into tears or whine in annoyance. But she didn't. Her heart whispered that this was all her fault. She would have to bear it like an adult and not panic.

"Can I go out in the sun now?" she asked, worried that this, too, would be refused.

"From eleven until two," Samara Orunbayeva explained, using her fingers to make things clear. "We live between two high mountains. The sun rises from behind one mountain and sets behind the other. That's how we live, my dear. And we're just fine. We aren't dead yet."

Erika looked out the window. She was trying to understand what Samara Orunbayeva had said when she noticed not the sun, but the old patched-up Moskvich from the day before.

"That car brought me here," she pointed in surprise and delight.

"My son brought you here from Bishkek."

"Oh! He is your son? I was rather afraid of him. Where is he now?"

Samara Orunbayeva paused for a second. She didn't know how to explain the delicate situation to a foreigner. But in any case she had to tell the truth, so that's what she decided to do. She started to tell the truth and nothing but the truth, as was the rule in Chet.

"Some of the assistants had already informed on him about you, my dear, so he went down to the border post to provide an explanation."

Erika said nothing, but her mouth was open. Her two big teeth and her freckled face made her look like a little girl. There were too many things she didn't understand and she was lost in thought, not even sure what questions to ask.

"It's alright. In time you'll understand. Just remember this: you are in Chet. Here everyone informs on everyone else. That's how people live here. You are the first foreign volunteer we've ever seen here. So be prepared. Soon they will drag you down to the border post like they drag everyone else. For questioning."

"What does 'questioning' mean?"

"The border guards will ask you everything they want to know. You must always speak and write the truth. Then they won't be able to do anything to you. If you write lies and get confused, they'll catch you. Then you'll have problems."

"What gives them the right to ask me anything?"

"It's a border post. The Government lets them do whatever they want in order to guard the border."

"Do they catch spies?"

"They catch anyone who illegally crosses the border."

"But I didn't illegally cross any border," Erika said with a forced smile.

"You're a volunteer. You're here legally. But who knows? So be very honest and tell the truth. The laws here are strict."

"Do the soldiers shoot people?"

"They do when they have to," Samara Orunbayeva said quickly. She could see by Erika's eyes that her head was spinning with thoughts of shooting and blood.

"I'm feeling very scared now." Erika wished that the older woman would give her a hug, but she didn't dare ask, so she sat down on a cot by the window.

"Don't be scared, angel. Everything will be fine. That's just how things are here. You'll be teaching our kids English just like you planned. Don't think about anything else."

"I hope to be studying the Kyrgyz language, too," Erika said cautiously.

***

According to the Chet school calendar, children went to school in the summer months and had the winter months off because the deep snow made roads impassable. Erika's first lesson with a group of eighth-graders was planned for June 4th, the first day of Childeh.[5] It was supposed to be a very important day for Erika: her first experience of teaching her very own class. She would be working with a new group of children she had never met before. She tossed and turned all night talking to herself.

"How do I say your first name? How do I pronounce your last name? Oh, that's very good. I'll now be able to remember your name well. You are now my very good friend. And you, how do I say your name, little girl? Aichurek! What a nice name. I really love that name. Aichurek is now my very good friend too. All of you are my very good friends. My name is Erika. Erika Klaus."

THE FOURTH STEP: OVERCAST SUN

Samara Orunbayeva took her to the school after lunch. The Principal, a man with a thick moustache named Soyuzbek Chabanov, was waiting for them in his office.

"They want to see our guest down at the border post. You have to take her there. Just this once. After that she'll go on her own," he told Samara Orunbayeva.

---

5 Childeh – (Kyrgyz) the hottest part of the summer according to the Kyrgyz Tengrian calendar.

Erika was standing behind the curriculum director. She didn't understand what the Principal was saying, so she expected Samara Orunbayeva to say something about what a big day this was for their new volunteer teacher. Her first lesson! This lofty thought made her pale face flush dark red.

Instead, Samara Orunbayeva glanced at the clock on the wall behind the Principal and said, "She could go to the border post after her first lesson. I'm sure they're not in a hurry."

"I can't tell them to follow my schedule. They already have me under suspicion. I had to provide a written explanation about her."

"Fine." Samara Orunbayeva immediately gave in. She took the surprised Erika out of the Principal's office.

"We'll have to put your first lesson off until tomorrow. I will send one of the other teachers to take your class so that you can go to the border post. For God's sake, be sure to write the truth. Answer all their questions honestly and then they won't be able to mess you about. Do you understand?" Samara Orunbayeva asked. She looked closely at Erika, studying her.

Erika overwhelmed by a terrible mixture of sadness and disappointment.. She turned her back to the school and started to dial the number of her friend in Bishkek. When the phone started beeping because there was no signal in the area, she didn't realize what it meant at first and kept waiting for her friend to pick up. Suddenly she changed her mind and turned off her mobile, realizing that as yet, there was nothing substantial for her to tell her friend. All she knew was that her first lesson had been postponed. She hadn't even been to the border post.

⁎

Based on the brief description from Samara Orunbayeva back at the house, Erika assumed that the border post was an office where honest people demanded honesty from everybody who came to see them. But once she saw the pitiful, helpless look of the Principal after he had run down to the border post to write an explanation about his foreign teacher, Erika felt less sure about this mysterious place. Apparently the people there were stern and powerful and you couldn't ask them to wait, even if you were anticipating the most important day of your life : your first lesson. The director hadn't wavered for an instant when he heard she was supposed to teach her first lesson. It was his indifference that hurt Erika most of all. But she had no time to think about that. She was already entering the border post.

She found herself staring at a metal door with a shiny red star over it. Under the star she saw marks made by a stick that had been used to scratch out a half-circle on the wall.

When she rang the bell, it tinkled out a little melody as if she had rung the bell of a kindergarten. A young man in a bright green military shirt and trousers of the same colour appeared in the doorway.

The soldier pointed to a room. When Erika went in, she saw that it was vacant. There was a table in each corner and a number of chairs. In a few minutes Erika heard a door open at the end of the hallway and loud voices talking. A minute later a young officer with green epaulettes on his shoulders and striking blue eyes walked into the room and stared at Erika.

"You're the chick we've been waiting for! We wanted to see what kind of beauty queen had made her way out here. We've never seen any foreign girls here before. Okay. Sit down."

Erika was always cautious around good looking men. She went so far as to avoid them because they usually didn't like pale girls and sometimes even laughed at them. She sat down on the chair, pointed to by the officer, and adopted a serious and slightly defensive expression. From the way the officer addressed her, she could tell that she wouldn't learn anything useful from him.

"Just look at you!" was his first response to her serious face. "Well, go on. Tell me what brought you to see me, beauty queen."

"I didn't come to see you!"

He laughed. "Okay. Then tell me who you came to see."

"The school. I'm a volunteer teacher. I teach English."

"Who do you teach? The other teachers?"

"Whoever wants to learn But first the children."

"They don't need English here. They need to learn Russian."

"First they need English."

"Who told you that? The Queen of England?"

"Egregor."

"Who? Did you say Egor?"

"Egregor!"

The sergeant hummed and hawed for a minute. He didn't know what she meant.

When he spoke again, his tone was friendlier:

"Explain who this Egrogor of yours is. I don't know him."

"It's not a person. It's the collective mind. It lives in space. It's a concept."

The sergeant's eyes widened. He didn't know what else to ask this pale girl in order to understand what she was talking about. Slowly, laughter appeared in his blue eyes. "Fine," he said, giving the impression that he was drawing their conversation to a close. Talking to her was becoming physically painful.

"Take our questionnaire and fill it out."

Just then a soldier peeked in and announced: There's some serious fighting going on!"

As the sergeant rushed out, he gave Erika instructions over his shoulder. "Don't rush!. Answer all the questions honestly and in detail. Then I'll come and check your answers."

***

It was late in the evening when Erika got home. The same young soldier who had opened the door for her showed her out. When Erika reached the yellow Moskvich the soldier handed her a piece of paper and hurried away. Sovietbek and Samara Orunbayeva were sitting in the car, still loaded with the textbooks it had brought all the way from Bishkek.

"I knew they'd keep you there a long time," exclaimed Samara Orunbayeva. She patted Erika on the shoulder as the girl climbed in beside her on the back seat.

"I hurt a lot," Erika answered. She covered her face with her hands. Samara Orunbayeva was not sure what she meant, so she leaned over and whispered in Erika's ear to keep Sovietbek from hearing. "Did they touch you?"

Erika uncovered her face and shook her head. "They took my passport."

"That's the rule, dear. They have all our passports. They didn't used to, but Kagan introduced a new law."

"But I can't leave now, can I?" Erika asked angrily.

"Why not? You can go if they give you permission."

"And how will that happen!?"

When they got home, Erika saw two teenage girls who looked very alike and seemed to be almost the same age. They were busy making dinner. When they saw Erika, they smiled broadly, even though they felt shy around the foreigner. Erika was not much taller than the two girls, both of whom had their hands covered with flour. They kissed each other's cheeks.

"I know you. You are Samara Orunbayeva's beautiful daughters; called...I think...Saikal and Aichurek. Kyrgyz names; adopted after Kyrgyzstan gained independence. So, now I'll teach you English and you will teach me Kyrgyz." Erika laughed. She was trying to shake off the bad mood she had brought home from the border post. It didn't work. When Samara Orunbayeva saw the blank questionnaire Erika had brought back with her, she grew concerned.

"Erika," she asked, "when are you supposed to take that form back?"

"Tomorrow after one o'clock."

"Not again! Your lesson is supposed to start at two-thirty."

"I'll complete it quickly and deliver it early morning."

"They won't accept it in the morning. If they told you after one o'clock, then that's when you hand it in."

Erika turned pale. "Do you think my lesson won't happen again?" She guessed what tomorrow would bring.

"If they let you go right away, then Sovietbek can bring you right back to school. But who knows what time they'll let you go?"

Protest welled up inside Erika. "I wrote so much today. Enough! I won't write more!"

"Do you mean you've already filled out a form like this today?"

"Yes. I speak Russian badly, and my written I Russian is worse, so I used English. They tore it up. They ordered me to write it in Russian so I wrote a lot in Russian. They said to write even more. I wrote some more. They said I had to complete this section properly."

She showed Samara Orunbayeva the form and pointed to "purpose of visit."

"What did you write there?"

"Volunteer teacher. I came to teach children English. That's what I wrote. They said 'That's an excuse. We want to know the purpose of your visit.' So I wrote exactly this 'the purpose of my life here is to teach children English.'

They laughed at me and shook their heads. They insisted it was an excuse. I don't know what they meant by that."

Erika looked at Samara Orunbayeva for an explanation.

"An excuse? I don't know how to explain it to you. I guess an excuse is like a reason. Well, let's ask Sovietbek. Soviet!" she yelled out the open window to her son, who was working on his car. "Come here! How would you explain the word 'excuse?' What does it mean?"

Sovietbek stood in the doorway wearing a black baseball cap and up to his elbows in motor oil. When he heard his mother's question, he snorted in surprise. He found a clean area on his hand and used it to rub his forehead while he thought.

"Why do you need to know?" he asked.

"Erika wrote on the form that she came here to teach children English."

"On what line?" Sovietbek asked quickly.

"Where it says *purpose of visit*".

"And then what?"

"They said that's just an excuse, not the real purpose of her visit."

"That means they're going to rake her over the coals."

Erika threw both hands up. "Why?" she asked.

"They don't believe you. An excuse is one thing, but they think you might have a totally different reason."

"Like what?" the girl yelled, almost crying.

Samara Orunbayeva broke in to calm Erika. "Don't worry, angel, just go to your room and take your time while you fill out the paper. Do you remember what answers you wrote on the other forms?"

"What other forms?" Erika dabbed the tears from her eyes.

"The ones you wrote earlier today."

"Yes."

"Then write the same things here. God forbid you write something different. They give people clean sheets to take home to see if they mix anything up."

Eagle Mother

That night Samara Orunbayeva realized that the following day would bring trouble. She could tell from the way the dog Kuchuk was barking loudly at everybody who crossed her territory and at her sleeping masters, as well.

Lying in bed with her daughters, the woman understood exactly why the dog was barking. For a long time she couldn't decide whether or not she should get up to see what was going on in the yard. She could hear footsteps and deep voices which disappeared behind the barn. That meant that some of Sovietbek's friends had come over. Eventually Kuchuk's barking lost its anger and anxiety and became a tired, infrequent woof. Samara Orunbayeva relaxed and was soon overcome by sleep.

The next morning, however, she woke up apprehensive. The sense of foreboding she had felt in the night took shape. When she ran out into the yard in her light summer robe she saw exactly what she had been afraid of. Her son was lying in his Moskvich with the doors open, drunk out of his mind. Two of his friends were lying in different directions behind the barn on Sovietbek's sunbed. Samara Orunbayeva looked closely at the drunkards' faces to see if there was any foam or vomit on their lips. She was concerned that they might have suffocated in a vodka-induced stupor. Her whole body filled with outrage: how was she supposed to bear this terrible drunkenness that had become commonplace among the men? She wanted to let loose a string of curses against the horrible baseness that was Chet, but something held her back. It must have been an instinctive impulse to forgive men for their animal-like behavior because she knew that when the women in Chet got together they drank far more and behaved worse than any of the men.

Samara Orunbayeva suddenly remembered Erika. She found a rag under the barn and used it to cover the doors of the car where her son was sleeping.

While Samara Orunbayeva was wondering where the young men had found money for vodka, the Akim[6] of Chet rode into the yard on horseback and told her that she was wanted immediately at the border post. When he turned his horse to leave, he called over his shoulder that she could pick up her bonus[7] while she was there.

"Alright, thanks. It's kind of early for it,"

"Ah, but it's only pennies. Less than last month."

"That's our fault. We can't be informing enough," Samara Orunbayeva replied ironically.

"It doesn't worry me. From now on, we'll be making money from your foreign girl" The Akim smiled as he spurred his big roan pacer.

***

The sound of the horse's hooves woke up one of the two men lying on the bed behind the barn. He held his right hand over his right eye for a long time and couldn't figure out that what he was feeling was blood seeping from the eyelid. As he rubbed the blood around his face, he kicked his friend in the hip and began to sit up and look over the empty bottles.

"Found it?" the other man asked, lifting his head and spitting out the phlegm that had collected in his throat.

"No. To hell with it. Let's go and take that eagle in."

"Fine with me. But you've got to bargain with that captain."

As they stumbled through Sovietbek's poor, weedy apple orchard, the one with the scratch on his right eyelid pointed at his eye and announced, "I'll ask him for a higher price because of this. The eagle's one thing, but what about my eye? That's something, too!"

"Who told you to let the eagle scratch your eye?"

"It was an accident, okay? The bitch caught me with her wing from quite a way off: Almost knocked me off the cliff!"

He turned his good eye to the cloudy mountain top where only the previous day the two of them had thrown a net over a mother eagle when she returned to the nest to feed her babies.

---

6 Akim – (Kyrgyz) head of the local independent government
7 Bonus – money paid by the border post to local residents for their "cooperation"

"The bald captain at the border post can try catching eagles for himself if he wants. He'd be dead in less than a minute!"

Around noon, when the two men with swollen faces and an eagle in their bag approached the border post, they saw that some strange sort of ceremony was being held on the parade ground, overgrown with spindly patches of grass. The flags at the gate flew at half-mast. The border guards were standing at attention, and parallel to them was a line of boys from the local school, led by Soyuzbek Chabanov and Samara Orunbayeva, both wearing black armbands. Several of the officers and sergeants also had mourning bands on their sleeves.

The man carrying the eagle in a bag over his shoulder stopped. "What the hell?"

"Who cares? One of their guys must've kicked the bucket."

"Then we'll wait. There goes the bald captain running around."

They sat down behind a bush and observed the scene at the parade ground. The soldiers brought a coffin adorned with a red ribbon out of the barracks and set it down in front of the head of the border post, who gave a eulogy.

"Our brave first-year fighter was killed in the line of duty. He was an exemplary soldier and had excellent military and political training. Private Simonov gave all he had to serve his country. Those who served with him, his sergeants and commanders will always remember him."

When the eulogy was over, the soldiers fired three times into the air. Then several soldiers carried the coffin to a helicopter waiting behind a stand of juniper bushes.

***

"Listen Comrade, are you going to buy it or not?" the man with the bag over his shoulder whined to the bald captain when they met amongst the weeds behind the border post.

"You idiot, didn't you just see the helicopter fly away?"

"So what?"

"What do you mean 'so what?' I can't hold the bird until the next flight."

"Then give us an advance, Comrade," the man with the bag begged.

"Have you brought the price down, or are you still asking ten rubles a bird?"

The second man broke in impatiently. "Just pay whatever you want!" The other man said nothing.

"Here. Let me take a look," said the captain said. He opened the mouth of the bag and peeked in. The mother eagle lay at the bottom of the bag with her head down and her neck twisted round. When he put the bag on the ground, she flapped her wings and tried to stand up. The bag was too narrow; no matter how hard she tried, the eagle could not right herself.

"Deal," said the captain. "And as an advance I'll pour you each a glass of hooch. Keep the bird for now. I'll tell you when to bring her in."

"Do you want us to catch some more, Comrade?"

"Catch as many as you want. Tell all your bird men that we'll raise the price a little for each bird. But you need to bring in more weed, and tell the others, too. It's less of a pain in the ass and you'll make good money."

"But yesterday, you only gave us ten rubles a box, Comrade," one of the men mumbled, sounding hurt.

"Stop crying, you greedy son of a bitch!" the captain spat at him. Then he led them down into the basement of an outbuilding.

***

The school in Chet was closed that day because the border post was in mourning.

***

THE FIFTH STEP: AN INSURGENT SUN

In the middle of the village was a patch of green grass where all week, a gaggle of boys had been noisily kicking around a football. That meant that their school was closed, an ostensibly sad fact that didn't seem to bother any of the teachers, much less the students. After sunbathing for two hours in the middle of the day, the residents of Chet disappeared back to their homes.

The only person who was truly concerned by the unexplained closure of the school was Erika. When she discovered that her eagerly anticipated first lesson was postponed for a third time and nobody knew when it might actually happen, the girl's face fell. She spent the rest of the day in her room with the door locked, crying without making a sound or shedding a tear.

All the insults and disappointments of the past two days overwhelmed her at once. Never seeing the sun, having her classes cancelled, and the rude treatment she received at the border post; none of these things were easy to bear and they weighed on her soul.

"Why was I so rude to my mother?" Erika asked herself bitterly. Unable to find an answer, she could no longer hold back her tears.

Then she began to wonder what she should do next. She had always been sure she could overcome any obstacle in order to reach her goal, and it was the goal she had chosen that gave her that certainty. Her goal was the most noble of all the goals her English teachers had set for her at university. Later she received confirmation of the rightness of her decision to become a volunteer teacher at the Emo club. The psychiatrists who had been invited to lecture at the club said the most wonderful things. They talked about the meaning of life for young people in Europe whose parents were well off, who had enough money in their own bank accounts to live on their own, and who, just for fun, took jobs doing things like working with travel agencies.

"That's no way to live," Erika had told her girlfriends on many occasions. "Well, it's life, but it's not real life. If you don't have a worthy goal, then your life is just a waste of time. You have to be useful to others if you want to have a clear conscience and not be disappointed in yourself."

By lunchtime she began comforting herself with the thought that if others could make a success of volunteer teaching, then so could she. She would just have to find the patience to deal with trouble as it arose. Everyone experiences problems at one time or another, don't they??

**

By evening she was ready to come out of her room if somebody knocked. Samara Orunbayeva's daughters were making *kesme*[8] and had promised to teach Erika how to cut the rolled dough into noodles. They should already have called her by now. Just then the knock came.

"*Ezheke*,[9] are you coming to make noodles?" one of the girls called.

Erika was enchanted the first time she saw how quickly the two girls turned mountains of thin, even dough into noodles, obviously not worried about cutting themselves with the sharp knife. It truly was an art form.

Erika kept jumping up and screeching for the girls to be careful. That made them laugh. Then they began to show off by chopping in a more dangerous manner, deliberately not watching their hands as the knife appeared to move automatically through the rolls of dough.

"Stop!" Erika cried out at one point, pulling Aichurek's hand away from the noodles. "I thought there was blood," she smiled, turning the girl's hand this way and that.

This time they rolled Erika a tube of dough so that she could cut some *kesme*. She spent a long time cutting the dough, putting her heart and soul into it. She even forgot for a while at least, about her troubles.

"Look! I've cut ten!" she smiled, pointing to a pile of crooked, uneven noodles.

**

Meanwhile, something had soured in the relationship between Samara Orunbayeva and her son Sovietbek. She always seemed to be pulling him up for some very serious offence or another, taking him aside into another room

8 Kesme – (Kyrgyz) Soup with noodles and shredded meat.
9 Ezheke – (Kyrgyz) Used to address an older girl.

and shouting at him. He always listened to her, but said nothing. This drove her to hysterical tears. At such moments, Erika, Saikal and Aichurek were afraid and stayed out of the way.

Then one day the contention between mother and son seemingly evaporated. Sovietbek, looking like a man in the throes of either fury or hurt feelings, went outside and threw himself into fixing up the abandoned two-room shed that stood by the house. A week later it was ready for use. No one but Samara Orunbayeva knew the reason behind the hasty repair job.

A few days later, she came to Erika and said, "Sweetheart, we're going to have boarders living in those two rooms. Don't worry about them. They won't bother us."

"Can I know who they are?"

"Travellers. There are a lot of people travelling these days, and they're all looking for lodging."

"What is lodging?"

"A place to sleep for the night. Just a room."

"I'm sorry for asking."

"Goodness no, dear, you're like a member of the family."

"Will Kuchuk bite them?"

"We'll tie him to the barn."

"Can I still go with the girls to Sovietbek's sunbed?"

"Of course, dear. It's yours, now. Sovietbek said so."

"How will he get the sun?"

"He'll find a way. He goes out with his friends a lot."

***

After lunch Erika went to find Samara Orunbayeva. "Samara-*apa*,"[10] she asked, sounding worried, "the girls say the Principal was arrested. I want to know, will the school continue?"

"My goodness, what big ears they have! They think they need to hear everything and spread everything around. Nobody arrested the Principal. They just locked the school and took the Principal to the border post. He's giving

---

10   Apa – (Kyrgyz) Used to address an older woman (meaning "mother")

his explanation down there about why he rented the empty half of the school to boarders. I guess they're fighting over the rent money. They'll work it all out."

"How long will it take?"

"He'll be back soon, and the school will open again. Don't worry, dear."

"Can I teach Saikal and Aichurek English at home?"

"Of course you can. That's the right thing to do. We can't do anything else for now, can we?"

"Thank you, Samara-apa."

Heartache

Sitting in lonely silence in the border post jail, for the umpteenth time Principal Soyuzbek Chabanov tried to work out a plan in his head to get rid of his longtime friend Bronza. He had several different options, but they all had the unfortunate drawback of liquidating the border post together with Bronza.

"That's no good!" he said out loud by accident, forgetting that he was sitting in a dark basement surrounded by peeping mice and a silent host of listening devices.

"That's no good for any of us," he continued, this time to himself. "Especially for me. If the border post is gone, it'll be lights out for Chet. Even if we take the tyrant out on our own, we'll be showing our cards. The Russians will remember about the border post and close it altogether. They've already shut up dozens of posts like ours and sent the guards to who knows where all over Russia. But our boy's a smart one! His head works like a whole committee. Before they closed his post he managed to sign an agreement with the Kyrgyz government to guard their side of the border for them. The country's poor enough. Of course they were happy to get free work out of the border post, so they hurriedly made Bronza a colonel. It's all a sham, but here's King Bronza sitting on his throne calling himself Kagan. Whenever anybody brings it up, he says 'We haven't received orders to demobilize.' And then he always adds 'If anybody spreads rumours about demobilization and can't show me the orders, I'll punish them to the extent of the law!' That's what he wants. Even if there is an order to demobilize, he doesn't want it to exist. Damn him! He's just Bronza. He punishes anyone who speaks the truth. Just like a black sorcerer: he blows in your face and, poof, you're gone!"

Soyuzbek Chabanov knew well and good that he would never do anything to Bronza, but he loved thinking about destroying him. One day he got so carried away with his dark plans that he forgot all caution and almost shared them with Sovietbek.

"Sovietbek," he began, finger to his lips, "he wants to bring back the same regime that we've already destroyed. Do you know what he said yesterday at the parade ground? He said 'You, the people of Chet, are just tiny little screws in a huge, living organism.' Do know who said that?"

They were facing each other on horseback in the middle of an empty field, but each of them knew that they would be obliged to run down to the border post and inform on the other. Knowing this, the Principal made a terrible mistake by letting his tongue run away with him in a moment of conspiratorial closeness.

Equally aware of the situation, Sovietbek glowered at him distrustfully and said nothing for a long time.

The Principal suddenly opened up. "I know you're on Bronza's black list because you're an *afganets*. You don't inform enough. That's why I'm being open with you."

"I don't inform much, and I don't trust any of you, either," Sovietbek said finally.

"But it's unbearable not to have anyone to share the pain with."

Sovietbek gave a crooked smile. "So you've got heartache?"

"Sovietbek, you're too smart to criticize a man for his past actions. We do what we do when we do it, based on current circumstances. Then we erase it from our minds. I'm no exception. Now let's think about how we can get out of this mess. As long as Kagan's in charge, we'll always be sitting in pig shit. And in the next life, they've got the worst corner of hell set aside for you and me, the one with the vampires and cannibals. Why? : Because you and I have lost our human dignity!"

"Money never stinks. We earn our money honestly and we tell the truth and nothing but the truth. Tomorrow we'll go and write about each other and get some sweet-smelling green paper in return. If we have to, we can even turn our brothers in. You'll see," Sovietbek said in a phony voice.

"I know you don't trust me, but I've changed since that time with my brother. If that's what you were referring to."

"I was referring to all of our brothers whom we've betrayed over eighty years."

"That's not our fault. The Communists set it a situation where there was no way out. We had no choice but to constantly turn people in."

"You and I are right up there with the *Pavliks and Kychan*."[11]

"You missed a few," the Principal said critically.

"The two of us had better go our separate ways. We can't be born again as new men this very minute. It won't work," Sovietbek spurred his horse and left.

The Principal watched the dark red back of Sovietbek's head fade into the distance. He was in two minds. On the one hand, he was relieved that he had not made the serious blunder of mentioning his plan to get rid of Bronza in front of the brave yet idiotic *afganets*. But on the other, his heart ached because he had spent his entire adult life living in such dirty, vile times. Everywhere he looked, people were doing the most monstrous things, and all in the name of "truth". It was depressing not to be able to talk about it openly with anyone.

***

Although the Principal gave the impression of being timid and tractable, he had a more obstinate side that emerged when he was cornered. So he sat patiently in jail waiting to see Bronza. He made no bones about being guilty. Yes, he had gone behind Bronza and rented out half the school to *"refugees"*[12] from the civil war in a neighboring country. The frightened "refugees" had been living in the classrooms for almost two weeks without showing their

---

11 *Pavlik and Kychan – children's book protagonists who betrayed their fathers in the name of Communism.*
12 *In most cases, drug traffickers pose as refugees.*

faces in daytime.

Yes, he had taken payment from them, and he was prepared to share it with Kagan which meant giving him the ninety percent that was his due and keeping ten percent of the profit for himself or rather, for the school.

"If any of our divisions arrest someone, and after he admits his guilt (in writing), the arrestee must go see the head of the border post. All violations of this rule will be punished."

Bronza had added this handwritten note to his thick border post instruction manual. Other than this Talmud there were no official laws in Chet.

Taking advantage of the current status of the border post, the Colonel took another clever step: he burned a huge pile of all the orders and instructions he had ever received from Moscow, down to the last scrap of paper. He then had the prudence to write up a report about a fire in the room where the orders had been kept. This freed him to write new governing *sharia*, just as prophets and tyrants have always done. The self-proclaimed ruler of everyone and everything in Chet did a good job of it, too.

***

Soyuzbek Chabanov had a hard time eating the runny porridge because his moustache got in the way. He was dismayed to find that in the damp basement where he sat, his moustache grew not only by the day, but by the hour. He tried to push his moustache to the side. Then he tried to twist it at both ends. Nothing worked. The hair was stiff as a hedgehog's spines. He considered himself to be an insider at the border post, so he asked a guard to bring him scissors or a knife so he could trim his moustache, but the soldiers pretended not to hear him. He then asked his wife to bring him an aluminum spoon so he could sharpen its handle against the cement wall and trim his moustache. His wife brought the spoon, but it was confiscated. Bronza's instructions only allowed for wooden utensils. He didn't want the inmates committing suicide.

"I'm going to complain! What right did he have to lock the whole school, and not just the empty half?" Soyuzbek grumbled to himself once he grew bored with his moustache problem. On second thoughts, this idea scared him.

"No, I can't ask Kagan what right he had. You can't catch him that way. He'll just grab me by the throat and say 'Everything I do, I do to protect the state borders and the people of Kyrgyzstan! What if your bearded renters, if that's what they really are, mine the whole school? Do you want all the children and teachers to get killed? Is that what you want?'"

Disappointed by his foolish idea, the Principal was trying to find some other accusation against Kagan when someone shouted his name and called "Take him to the Colonel!"

Soyuzbek Chabanov started at the unexpected command, but calmly made his way to the second floor where the head of the border post had his office.

Bronza, lean, head shaved and green eyes bulging, was seated at his desk. The dark brown holster he always wore was strapped to a belt over his left shoulder. Bronza used the commanding presence of his TT pistol to make up for the fact that he was not physically strong.

Soyuzbek Chabanov had been friends with Bronza for a long time and he knew he had an explosive temper. It was strange, but somehow the fits of anger always began internally: Bronza's neck would turn purple and his eyes would bulge out even further and turn blood red. While this was going on, the Colonel always managed to hold his tongue, restraining his usual profanity. The only other outward manifestation was the way he grabbed at his holster from time to time, almost, but not quite, pulling out the pistol.

During more peaceful conversations with people he didn't know, a disconcerting, snide, sneer occasionally appeared on his face and his eyes turned mysterious and probing.

"Sit down!" he pointed for his old friend Soyuzbek Chabanov to sit on a chair to one side, away from him.

"You've been in here for a while now. Got lice yet?"

"Not yet. Keep me a little bit longer and then maybe…"

"So you don't have lice yet. Well, how about a change of heart, you fool? Why have you been acting like your own boss? Have you forgotten how things work around here?"

"No."

"Then why are you making me mad?"

"You know why."

Bronza realized that their conversation might touch on personal matters, so he told the two bodyguards to wait outside.

"Get to the point. What do I know?"

"That I may hold a grudge against you."

"What for?"

"I'll tell you what for. Ainura's almost a wife to me and you know it, but you keep dragging her in here for yourself."

Bronza sniggered and stood up. He unbuttoned the top button of his shirt and adjusted his holster.

"How many wives do you have, you old bastard? Back in Soviet times I would have shot you for polygamy."

"I would have shot you, too. You have a whole harem!"

"But that's now. We have democracy now!"

"I don't give a shit about democracy. Don't touch my wives."

Bronza answered the Principal's angry look with a stern frown. "Give me the envelope and get the hell out of here."

"I'll give you your cut," Soyuzbek Chabanov said as he pulled an envelope from his shirt pocket, "but we'll lose the renters if you won't let me take them in. They'll go off to private homes."

"The private folks are more honest than you! I want full envelopes and not your pocket change. How much did you take from them? Don't lie!"

The Principal fidgeted in front of the Colonel like a schoolboy caught playing a prank. Then, grudgingly, he pulled out a cellophane bag as long as a belt. It was full of powdered hashish.

"I asked you how much you took them for!"

"How much do you think? They don't carry money with them. I took a third."

"You'd better be telling the truth."

As he left the office, Soyuzbek Chabanov had the impression that Bronza was not very angry at him, so he expected the Colonel to at least say a few friendly words in parting. The Colonel said nothing. His silence frightened the Principal more than anything, but when he walked home past the closed school he felt a deadly desire for revenge against his friend Bronza.

The empty school windows followed him like the eyes of an orphan, like a man with a gag in his mouth.

THE SIXTH STEP: WARM SUN

Sovietbek's next *bada*[13] fell on a Sunday. The sky was clear and the sun shone hot above the eastern mountain peaks, but it was not yet visible in Chet. The valley was still damp and cool, and drops of dew sparkled in the grass.

"Can I go and help Sovietbek?" Erika asked Samara Orunbayeva as they drank their morning tea.

"He won't be doing any real work up there," her hostess answered evasively.

"Then I could watch the baby goats play. I think they're adorable."

Samara Orunbayeva looked at her two daughters. Perhaps they would go, too?

"We have the washing to do, Mother."

Sovietbek put on his old, broad straw hat and followed the sheep, who were led by two white goats and their kids along paths that only they knew.

Erika caught up with Sovietbek. Her voice was happy. "Samara-apa said I can come too. I love herding the baby goats."

"Oh, they're pretty fast. They'll be fine without you."

"This is my first day as a shepherd!"

"Congratulations."

Erika was walking through the wet grass in sandals. Her bare legs were wet to the knees and the sores on her skin began to ache. They hurt so much that she almost cried.

Sovietbek led the girl to a dry path and gave her his jacket to dry her legs.

"Is that better? he asked.

"A little bit."

---

13 Bada – (Kyrgyz) rotation among neighbors who herd their sheep together.

"The pain will go away soon. You should be patient and walk in the wet grass more often. Then you wouldn't have any sores at all."

"So the dew is also medicinal?"

"Every piece of grass and every flower is a medicine. You just have to know what they treat."

While they were talking, the two goats made a sharp turn toward the rocky foothills and the sheep merrily followed along behind.

Erika was worried. "They've gone the wrong way!"

"The goats know what they're doing. It's pointless trying to herd them. They always lead the flock to where the grass is juiciest."

"What do you mean by juiciest?"

"Sweet. Good tasting."

"Oh. So the goats are smarter than the ram?"

"Of course. The ram is just a ram. Goats are like girls, and rams are like boys."

" You should be embarrassed talking like that !" Erika laughed, covering her two big front teeth with her hand.

"The sun is drying the dew. Try walking through the grass again," Sovietbek told her.

A little while later, after the four goats had had enough to eat, they began to play, leaping from rock to rock. Erika watched them raptly as they chased each other over the rocks. She got as close to them as she could.

"Won't they fall?" she asked, watching with concern as the goats jumped higher up the rocks.

"No. Their hooves are soft. They hold the rock like rubber."

Erika kept watching the eastern mountains in expectation of the sun. Finally it appeared.

She turned to Sovietbek for permission. "May I sunbathe without my clothes?"

He shrugged, "Hey, it's a free country," and walked off.

Erika quickly removed her t-shirt, bra and skirt, leaving only her skimpy underwear. She spread her clothes on the grass and lay down on her back to soak up the sun's ultraviolet rays.

When the sun disappeared, Erika lay a little while longer and then jumped up like a toy on a spring. She hurriedly got dressed and began looking for Sovietbek. He was lying between two nearby bushes with his shirt off. Even though his skin was dark, his hairy shoulders and chest were slightly sunburned. The sight of a strapping man's naked torso excited Erika, and in true Emo Club fashion she called out the first thing that came into her head.

"Sovietbek, do you have sex?"

Sovietbek turned to face the girl and said nothing.

"Did you understand what I said?"

"Yeah," he answered dryly.

Erika shrugged her shoulders and dropped down onto the grass. She studied the bright red mountain poppies. The soft, thin petals of the poppies with their wonderful patterns delighted her, but her ears were straining to hear Sovietbek say something. He remained silent. Soon he came over to her and sat down.

"These are poppies, right?" she asked for clarification.

"That's right. Mountain poppies," Sovietbek said with a warm smile.

Erika put her chin on her knees and stroked the petal of a rich, red poppy until it fell off.

"Oh!" she cried. "That's a bad sign, right?"

"No, it isn't. The petals are very delicate. Soon a light breeze will blow this whole field of red petals away."

"Why? That's too bad!"

"It only takes them a day or two to get pollinated, and then it's all over."

"Pollinate? What is that?"

"Let me see. It's a form of reproduction. With animals it's called mating. It's how those baby goats were made."

"Ah, like children? I see. Do you love children?"

"Of course I do."

While they were talking, Erika hadn't forgotten the question she had asked Sovietbek about sex. It offended her that he had ignored her. If he didn't want to talk about it, then he could just have made a joke. This feeling of being affronted prodded Erika to take another step.

She decided to apologize with a hint of sarcasm in her voice. "I did a bad thing. I joked about sex. Can you forgive me?"

Sovietbek blushed. He snorted and was about to say something, but then stopped and hung his head.

"People here are not allowed to talk about this kind of thing. I forgot. Can you forgive me?"

"That's not it. We're learning from the West. We have everything you have: hits, hops, Emos, porn clubs, bars with drugs. So I understand you all the way. Teenagers in the city, even out here in the countryside, could show your teenagers a thing or two."

Erika was genuinely surprised. "So you have the same stuff going on here as in the West?"

"What did you expect? Internet, DVDs, television. Everyone has mobile phones and they all go to clubs. Everything here is the same as what you have there. Even worse!

Erika gave him a friendly smile and asked, "So you don't like it?"

"I'm an *afganets*. I'm broken. I have other problems to worry about. My own problems! All I'm worried about is the fascists. You know why? Because I was a fascist once. I killed people!"

Erika's eyes widened and her face grew tight. As usual, she wanted to ask him direct questions; "You are a fascist? You killed someone?", but she was afraid of the answers. She stared at Sovietbek, making no attempt to hide her fear. His lips were trembling and his hands shook, betraying the signs of the concussion he had sustained in Afghanistan, something he had managed to hide from the other people in Chet.

***

The sun sank behind the mountains. With the arrival of the cool evening air, the sheep grew more animated.

Erika was the first to break the gloomy silence. "Why do we have to watch them? They aren't afraid of anything, are they?"

After a minute, Sovietbek lifted his blank eyes to her face. "What did you

say?"
 "The rams are afraid of nothing, right?"
 "They are afraid of wolves."
 "Where are the wolves?"
 "Far from here."
 "Then why are they afraid?"
 "People are wolves. Strangers come and chase our animals over the border ,then make us pay to get them back."
 "What people?"

The Poisonous Viper

As the helicopter carried him along his usual control route, Bronza's experienced eye estimated how many people, cars, trucks, other vehicles, horses, mules and donkeys were making their way through his border crossings. He had five crossings, three of which he kept a close eye on. These were the crossings where he focused on stopping the drug trade and shipments of illegal weapons and military supplies headed for the terrorist groups that made their way over the border from the East. He also caught slave traders who pretended to be illegals or migrant workers.

Bronza's trusty ensigns and sergeants checked people's documents, patted down the clients and processed payments under the watchful eyes of one or two officers stationed in camouflaged, lightweight aluminum and plastic structures that were easy to disassemble and move. If necessary, they could be broken down in less than half an hour, leaving not a single trace of Bronza's border crossings.

Bronza had issued Ural motorcycles to three officers and charged them with collecting the cash and other forms of profit on a daily basis. The cash collectors were escorted on their rounds by special bodyguards chosen from Bronza's best turds, and a sniper division covered every step of the road they travelled.

The cash collectors, led by Bronza's top men, frequently ended up in chases and shoot-outs with groups of bandits illegally crossing the border. For this reason, all the border units and other forces received their orders from Colonel Bronza in strict military fashion on the parade ground, with all the soldiers looking on, and most importantly under the two nations' flags, which flew on poles in front of the border post headquarters. It was here ,each Monday, that the most important orders were read aloud and the finest border guards received medals and certificates "for excellence in protecting the nation's borders" or "for praiseworthy border service" of the first, second and third orders.

Bronza had recently instituted a new medal that the officers and men coveted more than all others because it always came with a large sum of money in a sealed envelope. The residents of Chet also dreamed of being awarded the Bronza medal for dedicated service to the fatherland. After all, the medal was sometimes bestowed on civilians but only the most active of the volunteers, of course.

***

With his head newly shaved and dressed in the rough, bright green shirt and trousers of a Private for security's sake, Bronza cautiously crept upstream along the bank of the Chet River. Orchid flowers poked out of the grass here and there like the tips of purple arrows. Out of curiosity Bronza picked a few of the flowers. He was about to sample their scent when he saw a line of women with bags on their backs making their way through the underbrush, along the slope. There were about twenty of them, the usual number, and they were either migrant workers or "refugees." Bronza crouched in the bushes and found himself eyeing the wind-blown, half-naked women walking through the wilderness, wondering whether any of them were worth his attention. There was one! But she looked like she hadn't bathed in ages, and her skin was grimy with dirt and sweat. Then he noticed a thin, half-naked boy of about twelve. Bronza stared at the playful swaying of the boy's buttocks and immediately felt the blood rush to his head and groin.

"I bet they'll spend the night in Chet, but not at the school with that ass

Soyuzbek. I'll find that boy anyway," he thought as he headed up along his trail. When he reached the border zone of juniper bushes he sat down for a long wait. He lifted his binoculars and began observing how his border crossings looked from behind the lines.

Some of the crossings were taking too long to let people through.

"That means my donkeys are haggling with folks, trying to raise the price!" the Colonel growled. "That doesn't do me any good because they'll hide the extra money from me anyway. And they slow people down. When people get tired of waiting, they'll leave and go through the official border crossings. It costs them the same, but they get through faster, without queuing. That hurts my business!"

Bronza reviewed all of his crossings and then set off on the real business, unbeknown to anyone, that had brought him there,

The people of Chet called the place where Bronza now sat on a stone, legs tucked under him, "snake ordo."[14] For as long as anyone could remember, poisonous vipers had nested up there in the rocks. When the ground was warm in the summer, they crawled out in their hundreds and spread out over the high plateau in search of food. Most of the time, however, they stayed near their nest, and that was the best place to find them. That was what Bronza had come for. He took thick spiraea branches and made them into a long, forked stick. Then, step by cautious step, he began pushing back the thick bushes in search of the snake he wanted.

The hunt had been preceded by a week of a familiar depression that sometimes afflicted Bronza. His lungs couldn't get enough air, his hands and feet grew weak and his whole body felt heavy. It felt as if the blood in his veins was slowing and thickening.

"When you feel that way, you have to clean your blood," an old Kyrgyz hunter named Mergen had told him when he first came to run the border post many years ago. "And if your manhood lets you down, you have to get the gall bladder of a wild sheep and eat it while it's still warm."

The search did not take long. After a few steps, Bronza caught a yellow-bellied viper by the tail and held its head down with his forked stick. Then, in one swift motion, he cut off the snake's head and stuffed its bloody

14 Ordo – (Kyrgyz) gathering, center

body into his mouth, preventing any of the blood from dripping onto the ground. The colonel closed his eyes as he chewed then swallowed the bland, barely warm body of the poisonous snake. He was pleased to feel the healing fluid with its magical properties infiltrate his heavy body through thousands of tiny capillaries.

Later that evening, after dinner and a heavy dose of Armenian brandy, Bronza thought about the boy he had seen that day in the hills and who had been on his mind ever since. The boy would be found in Chet, brought to the border post and thoroughly washed. Even affairs of this sort were well organized by the boss.

Soon the wide-eyed, curly-headed boy walked into Bronza's spacious rooms. The boy was prepared to be friendly with this seemingly generous, funny old man who might give him expensive presents, so he was not intimidated by the unfamiliar surroundings and smiled widely at the old man with the bald head and moustache.

The boy did receive an expensive present: a mobile phone with earphones. At first he didn't wonder what the present was for, but when the old man started doing strange things the boy recoiled sharply and began to fight like a man, hitting and kicking, even butting with his head.

There had been a time when Bronza had tolerated this type of defiance and was willing to spend the time necessary to pacify his victims. That was no longer the case. Enraged by the boy's fighting spirit, he took out his Taser and aimed at the naked skin of the boy's chest. A second later, the colonel's victim was on the floor, disoriented and clutching the side of the bed to keep himself from falling.

The colonel only discovered the boy's lifeless body next to him in his queen-sized bed when, very drunk, he woke up in the middle of the night and tried to satisfy his cravings again. The boy's body was already cold and stiff and the sheets beneath him were covered with blood. Sitting in bed next to the body, the colonel couldn't gather together his thoughts for a long time. Under the strong influence of alcohol, snatches of the night's events broke through the fog in his mind, only to disappear again. Most of all he wanted to sleep, to forget everything. His leaden head was pulled toward the pillow. It called him to a dead man's sleep. He had just decided that was what he would do when he suddenly saw the boy's twisted body on his bed. What should he do?

The colonel's hazy eyes fixed on the shadowy outline of his bedroom window. Swaying from side to side, he got up, took the dead boy by the legs and held him out the window. He swung the body back and forth for momentum, and then threw it as hard as he could towards the other end of the building.

The colonel slept late. When he awoke, he didn't call for coffee until he had taken the time to put himself and his chaotic thoughts in order. When a soldier silently entered his room, he looked into the man's eyes to see if they held any sign of the night's troubles. There was none. Bronza immediately relaxed and picked up his coffee.

He then went to his office and settled himself behind his desk. There was a knock at the door. It was Major Sidorov, Bronza's deputy for operations.

"Allow me to report, sir!"

"Let's hear it!"

"Last night, between four and five in the morning, the body of an unidentified boy was discovered outside the second entrance of building number one. There were no signs that he had been beaten or stabbed."

"Who was the boy?" Bronza asked loudly.

"Apparently he was one of those illegals. His mother came looking for him. She's in a pretty bad state. She knows he's dead. She wants to see you, sir!"

"Where is the body?"

"It's in the cooler for now. We are awaiting your orders, sir! And what do you want me to do with the boy's mother, sir?"

"Lock her up for three days. Charge her with illegally crossing the state border. Once she's had a change of heart, have her sign an affidavit that she has no complaint against the border post. Then toss her back over the border."

"What about the body, sir?"

"We cremate unidentified bodies!"

"Yes sir! May I go?"

"Go!"

As he left Bronza's office, Major Sidorov clicked his heels together and reflected on the sizeable reward he would receive for following the colonel's orders and hushing up the affair, even though he knew exactly where the body had come from. Everybody at the border post knew that situations of this sort resulted in a generous reward from the boss. That thought lifted the heart of every soldier.

A Pretty Girl

Chet society, like any other, experienced a whole range of community events, from funerals and weddings to drunken rages, fistfights and holidays. There were also long stretches of dark days when it seemed that nothing good could happen.

On one of those grey days, people's imaginations were fired up by a piece of unexpected news that instantly raced through the *aul*. Neighbors hurried to tell other neighbors that one of Chet's young men, a fellow by the name of Askarbek,[15] had brought home a very pretty wife. What made the situation tricky was that people immediately began to discuss where the bride was from. At first Askarbek said that his young wife was from the nearby village of Pokrovka. Others claimed he told them that he brought her home from Bishkek. The groom's parents either stayed silent on the matter or avoided the discussion entirely.

In light of the confusion, it was no surprise that the border post was soon made aware of the rumours. The border guards had a strict policy of maintaining their informers' confidentiality, so when Askarbek was called to the Post he was not sure at first who had informed on him. This was not usually a difficult matter for the residents of Chet. Most of the time, most people knew perfectly well who had informed on them, based on what information the Post had been given.

Chet and the Post had been working closely together for so many years that they had eventually come to an understanding on the exact number of signals each "volunteer" should submit per month: an average of six outside signals and three inside signals. For some reason, Bronza had recently changed

15 *Askarbek – A Kyrgyz name that means "Red Army soldier"*

this to just one outside signal and six inside signals. Outside signals were defined as information about illegal border crossings by people, animals or objects. Inside signals were also indirectly related to guarding the border, but they came from closer to home and involved the moral, political, psychological, patriotic or other emotions of each person in the border village.

Askarbek had been a volunteer for years, but as he headed to the Post he kicked himself for the fact that this time he had behaved stupidly, like a boy who was still wet behind the ears. Any sergeant could crack the case in an instant. Every move he made would be painfully obvious.

He walked into the Post with a heavy heart and was received by the sergeant on duty. Although he knew several handlers among the officers, he did not try to get special treatment. The longer you can't get something, the more you want it. That is just what had happened to Askarbek. He had spent five or six years wrangling with Afghan authorities to get permission for his beloved to leave the country, but when they finally gave permission he made a dumb mistake.

"Sit down and talk," ordered a young sergeant whom Askarbek had not seen before. His face was severe and he looked ready to confront the problem of the bride's provenance, full on. Askarbek sat down on a chair. A few minutes into the conversation he realized that the young sergeant was aiming at something completely different. He was insinuating that Askarbek had stolen his bride and that she did not want to marry him. "You should be ashamed of yourself for stealing a woman in this day and age. When will you Kyrgyz ever give up these wild customs?"

Askarbek's eyes slowly brightened and he promised the sergeant that he would bring a note from his wife testifying that the situation was the opposite of what the Post feared.

After Askarbek returned home from the Post in a jovial, elevated mood, his neighbours and close relatives cast off their fears and headed over to his house to congratulate his parents on the appearance of a daughter-in-law.[16]

"May the leash on your young falcon be strong," Askarbek's aunt gave the traditional greeting as she embraced her sister and her sister's husband.

Then she opened a large cloth, revealing freshly cooked *boorsaki*[17] and clar-

16 In Kyrgyz tradition, a wedding is a time for congratulating the newlyweds' parents, less so the newlyweds themselves.
17 Boorsaki – yeasted dough that is rolled out thinly, sliced and fried in butter.

ified butter. She put a white silk scarf on the bride's head and voiced the traditional hope that the newlyweds would always have countless livestock grazing in front of them and a whole pack of children running behind them.

***

Three days later Askarbek's affairs took a sharp turn for the worse. He was not called back to the Post, but a group of riders, two soldiers and Soyuzbek Chabanov, Askarbek's brother, was put together and charged with discovering the truth about where the bride had come from. When Askarbek heard this news from his secret sources, he immediately went to see his brother. Soyuzbek was dressed for a long trip and was already saddling his bay stallion, admired in the *aul* for its strength and speed.

Askarbek stood at the gate, his face pale. "*Baike*,[18] where are you headed this early in the morning?" he asked.

"On business," Soyuzbek answered as he spurred his horse.

Askarbek had to jump back to avoid being trampled. His brother's behaviour cut him to the quick and he called after him as loudly as he could, "Baike! I know why you're going. When you come home, I'll shoot you and Allah will forgive me."

Soyuzbek had not wanted to turn around, but when he heard the name of Allah he reined in his horse and turned back. "I kept my mouth shut while you earned cash from my troubles, so now you shut yours!"

***

Soon the mounted soldiers, led by the Principal of the school, discovered that Askarbek had not brought his wife from Bishkek or some other far-off place, but rather, from right next door, in Afghanistan. The pair had come through the Chet valley and crossed the border illegally. Up in the hills the soldiers found a homemade inflatable *sal*[19] lying in the bushes not far from the Chet River. This was how the lovers had crossed the river in the middle of the night.

***

18 Baike – (Kyrgyz) used to address an older brother
19 Sal – (Kyrgyz) raft

The bride's name was Gulchakhra. She came from a Kyrgyz family in Afghanistan and had corresponded with Askarbek over the internet for two or three years. They had exchanged photographs, and then Askarbek saw Gulchakhra in person on one occasion when he had legally crossed into Afghanistan on a truck driver's visa.

When he met Gulchakhra, Askarbek became timid. Deep in his heart he was sorry he had come, because in real life Gulchakhra turned out to be very beautiful and dignified. Askarbek was ashamed of the pitiful, retouched photograph of Gulchakhra which he had admired online.

He felt that all of the sincere things which he had composed to say to her, as he lay awake at night, were now just empty sounds. Gulchakhra stood before him, one hand on the gate, like a real, live goddess whose beauty was beyond any words or retouched images. Askarbek realized that he had been struggling to climb a peak that he was not meant to reach. He expected to see the light in Gulchakhra's warm, brown eyes go out as she realized that she had been duped by her virtual suitor.

But Askarbek's luck was still good. The girl saw a small, skinny man with a wrinkled face, but her eyes were still kind and welcoming. Askarbek was at a loss to understand why.

He learned the reason later when he sat with Gulchakhra's father, his legs under the round table.

"My dear son, all of the Kyrgyz in Afghanistan dream of returning home to the Alatoo.[20] Only our bodies are here. Our souls are in our homeland. Our hearts dream of the great *Alatoo* and the miraculous *Issyk-Kul.*[21]

"Back home people say that you left the Alatoo because you didn't want to live under the Soviets," Askarbek ventured cautiously.

"That's all lies, son! That spring our fathers left their *auls* as they did every year, to take their livestock to summer pastures. The season lasts until autumn. By the time they came back from their far-off mountain pastures, the Soviets had built a border post in Chet and they could go no further. In the end, Russian soldiers began shooting at the Kyrgyz who tried to come home. That's how we ended up homeless between Afghanistan and the USSR. Eventually

20 Alatoo – name of a major mountain range in Kyrgyzstan
21 Issyk-Kul – name of a large lake in Kyrgyzstan

the Afghan government gave us official asylum, but they told us not to come down from our mountain pastures. We were grateful to them, even though half of us died from the terrible cold.

"That is why we treat any Kyrgyz from the homeland as our own blood, son. My heart is weak and I am not supposed to get upset, but I wrote a poem about the pain in my soul. You may read it if you want."

> *I would rather be a black crow*
> *Than a stranger in someone else's land.*
> *I would fly through barbed nets*
> *Just to warm myself in the smoke of my homeland.*
> I would rather be a fish without a tongue
> Than be born without a home.
> I would swim through barbed nets
> To the clear lakes of my own high mountains.
> I am past sixty years now,
> But I have no woman to love to the end.
> To be born and die like an ant,
> That is the fate that was handed to me.

When Gulchakhra's father had finished reading the strange poem, Askarbek looked at him in silence. He was not sure whether or not to believe that the old man had really written it. The old man sat with his chin on his chest. Askarbek did not dare ask about the poem's true origins. Just then, the door opened and the lovely Gulchakhra came in.

She smiled when she saw that her father's guest was confused. "How do you like my father's poem?"

Looking into the girl's eyes, Askarbek realized that the poem expressed her father's years of mourning for his home and his endless grief. It was more than his heart could understand. What could make a man no longer want to be a man, but turn into a fish or even a crow? This is what the people who had lost their home had felt for over a century, ever since the damned Red border post had come to Chet.

"But we are an independent state now! Why don't you ask the Kyrgyz government for permission to return home?" Askarbek asked. Before he had finished his question, he saw by the old man's reaction that the answer would be discouraging. And it was.

Based on a survey of the residents of Chet, your request to relocate to Kyrgyzstan cannot be approved due to the fact that all of the Kyrgyz minors in Afghanistan are addicted to drugs and would require treatment for sexually transmitted diseases.

Sincere best wishes, the Minister of Foreign Affairs, Kyrgyz Republic

It was hard for Askarbek to believe what he had just read, even though he held the paper in his hands. This was the response of the Minister. The young man reflected on the fact that there were complicated problems in this world, many of which he had never even heard of, which were beyond his ability to comprehend,

Gulchakhra stuck her head out of the kitchen. "Ata, it's time to wash our hands. Dinner is ready."

"Of course, daughter. We have waited long enough."

Gulchakhra came in carrying a teapot in one hand and a towel over her shoulder. She began to pour water over their hands.

"Thank you, daughter. May you live to an old age with your chosen man," he said, thanking her as was the custom. When Gulchakhra poured water over Askarbek's hands, his ears turned a firey red. He saw that his hands were ugly, black and bony. Why had he never noticed before?

When it was time to thank Gulchakhra, all he could say was one word , "thanks" , even though as a guest ,he was supposed to say "May Allah give you all that you wish for." He was afraid of saying what he ought, because he thought it would make him appear a puffed-up fool.

The surprise came the next morning, when Gulchakhra's father turned to Askarbek with the same pained expression as he had had during the reading of his poem and said, "My son, it is an honor for us to join blood with our brothers from Alatoo. Therefore I give you my permission to remain in my home and perform the *kuyoloo*[22] ritual.

Askarbek began to sweat. He had been planning to run away from Gulchakhra after breakfast. He wiped his forehead with his hand. It was hard

---

22 During kuyoloo, the groom lives at the bride's house for nine or 12 days in order to receive consent from her parents and relatives for them to marry. During this time he must show himself to be worthy in all respects.

for him to make the mental leap from being not worthy of Gulchakhra to deserving her hand. His answer immediately revealed his embarrassment and helplessness.

"The Post doesn't let us do kuyoloo.

"Who?"

"The Post."

Gulchakhra's father did not know what to say. He knew what the Post was, but what his future son-in-law had just said made absolutely no sense to him.

"The Post refuses to let people get married?"

"Yes. I mean no. You can."

"I don't understand what the problem is, son!"

"They won't let us get married the old way."

"What is the new way?"

"We have to get their permission."

"*Kokuy! Kokuy!*"[23] Gulchakhra's father put his head in his hands and said nothing for a long time.

Then he regained his self-control and spoke quietly. "Do not listen to the Post. We are two Kyrgyz brothers who have been kept apart. We must be joined. I will leave this life soon, so I want you to tie yourselves to each other with the bonds of marriage, my children. Otherwise our people will disappear. The strong always think that the weak are at fault. We can bear this, because in heaven or in hell, the strong always live one less day than the weak. That is how Allah created us. It is a sign of his eternal justice! *Assalaamu 'Aleykum*![24] Have a safe trip, my children. Go and find your happiness!"

✳✳✳

Trapped by the incontrovertible evidence against them, Askarbek and Gulchakhra who had been married by the local mullah on their first night home, were arrested and jailed at the Post. They were questioned, ostensibly to obtain a confession. Bronza wanted to finish the investigation as soon as possible and use it to shame the Afghans and put a shine on his tenure at the

---

23 *Exclamation expressing distress*
24 *Assalaamu 'Aleykum – Arabic greeting that means Peace be upon you.*

Post where he was successfully managing the drug trade.

They didn't take long to finish with Askarbek. He admitted everything. But one officer after another dragged out the questioning of his wife. They said it was impossible to question her because she did not speak Russian.

"Why are you letting her off easy? Send her to me!" he ordered his deputy in charge of operations.

"The interpreter is sick, sir!"

"You goddamn idiot! Half the *aul* can interpret. Call in one of them or I'll do it myself!"

They soon brought Gulchakhra to the head of the Post. He had read all the documents on her arrest. The newlyweds had been arrested on the basis of information provided by the groom's own brother, Soyuzbek Chabanov.

"Son of a bitch," Bronza thought with a scornful smile. "He wants to make some money off his brother. The bastard doesn't want me touching his wives, but he's happy to shove his brother's wife at me!" Despite these thoughts, Colonel Bronza was prepared to greet the young Gulchakhra politely. He assumed that the other officers had been openly rude and lustful in their exchanges with her.

However, judging by the young woman's first reaction to his supposedly friendly smile, he realized that he had been mistaken. Gulchakhra's eyes answered the colonel's fake smile with open enmity. She reacted to the words, gestures and expressions of the man in front of her like a scared child, too young to talk. When the colonel tried speaking to her in broken Kyrgyz without asking any questions for the moment, she reacted with revulsion to his every word and her beautiful brown eyes filled with tears. And when Bronza's gaze lowered ever so accidentally to her full, round breasts, she grabbed the neck of her dress to protect her neck and bosom from his greedy eyes. He knew that if he ventured to accuse her of anything, she would cry so hard that he wouldn't be able to stop her. Realizing this, the colonel's face grew stern. Gulchakhra's eyes widened with fear. Her face paled as she watched for him to make even the slightest movement.

The colonel was about to curse at the wild woman, as he now considered her, but his sense of official duty and the unusual beauty of the strange young girl held him back.

This was something out of the despotic officer's realms of experience; standing before him, was a pure girl from a Muslim family who had never been to a nightclub or watched porn on television or video. From girlhood, she had been taught that non-Muslims were *kafuryi* because they ate pork and that Russians were the worst of them. She was supposed to go out of her way to avoid them altogether, much less speak to them.

Forced to stand in close proximity to *kafury* for the first time, Gulchakhra was terrified that one of them might touch her body. That would have been a terrible sin; bad enough to prevent a Muslim from entering heaven.

After staring at Gulchakhra as if she were a trapped beast, the colonel realized that he had nothing to say to her. However, there was one thing he knew for sure: he would bring her to his bed that night. He couldn't think of anything else to do with her, and it would have been a shame to pass up the opportunity.

He spoke into his handheld radio, "Have her ready for an interview with me this evening!"

***

The Colonel's evenings were lively, sometimes lasting well into the night, and they always gave him a great deal of pleasure.

When his officers were finished with the day's work at the border crossings, they came in to report to Kagan. The procedure was for the heads of each border crossing to hand over to Kagan, all their money and the day's confiscated valuables, including gold, silver, diamonds, pearls, explosives, guns, knives and whatever else there was. Everybody enjoyed the procedure. Bronza accepted the items happily, often with arms outstretched, and gifted his underlings with a fraction of the "profits."

"I love honesty and truth," he always repeated at the end of the ceremony. "If any of you try any funny business or try to hide something from me, I promise you'll be sorry! Truth and honesty are our guiding principles!"

"We are happy to work hard, sir! We will follow you to the end!" That was how his underlings answered him after he had shared the profits every evening.

When Bronza was finally alone in his office, he opened his safe and took out the saber with the gold handle encrusted with diamonds which he had just received. The saber had been confiscated from a Chinese businessman who was trying to get into Russia through Kyrgyzstan at one of the crossings.

Bronza admired the saber. He touched it to test the sharpness of the steel. He then had a bold idea. With one swipe, he cut the head off the plaster bust of the current President that stood on his desk. Then he cut off the head of a second President, the one he was supposedly serving at the same time.

"The End!" he exclaimed. He looked at the white plaster heads lying on the floor. The heads were not real, but all of a sudden Bronza subconsciously felt that he had done something potentially rather dangerous. He quickly located an empty cardboard box, put the broken plaster busts in it and hid it in the back of a cabinet.

Afterwards, he went back to thinking about Gulchakhra. He had thought about her several times that day. At first he had been inclined to think kindly of her. He had even considered giving her one of his expensive baubles. But when he saw how hard the sergeants had to work to pull her into his room, he turned cold. The "wild woman's" eyes were bloodshot, just like the eyes of an enraged predator. Her face was scratched and bruised. Her hair was so tangled that he knew they had pulled her by the hair to get her there.

Bronza was so infuriated by this scene that his blood began to boil. His face turned purple and his bulging eyes turned red.

"Why is the bitch fighting like that?" he yelled. He was offended that a country girl would protest so vehemently against the "inoffensive" desires of his powerful ego. She did not know who it was they were taking her to. The fool did not know who it was who wanted to stroke her womanly body. She didn't care! She had no regard for Bronza at all! He was hurt.

"Put her in solitary. Don't feed her and let her breathe *milk*[25] for three days," he ordered, his whole body shaking. He wanted to put a harsh, pitiless stop to her ignorant disdain for him. He would have none of this in the future!

25 *Milk – fumes of ammonium and opium*

THE SEVENTH STEP: KIND SUN

Erika lay sunning herself on the bed Sovietbek had put together. She was wearing nothing but thong underwear. Samara Orunbayeva's daughters, Saikal and Aichurke, lay on their backs next to her. Erika had talked them into undressing like she did so that they could soak up even more of the sun's rays.

The girls giggled as they repeated English words after Erika, trying not to look around. They were perfectly aware that the village children were watching them from behind the bushes and trees. Aichurek and Saikal were absolutely absorbed in this inoffensive activity because even though they were still children, they had the instincts of young women. They did not think of it in so many words, but they wanted to show the boys their young bodies and budding breasts. Meanwhile, they tried to steal glimpses of those parts of the boys that were off limits to them. It all seemed like a game between children.

Erika, however, was weighed down by low spirits. She had decided that this was caused by her sudden break with everything she had ever known, the complete lack of certainty about what was to come, and her defenselessness against the inexplicable and unbelievable behaviour of the border guards.

"I can't believe they just closed the school. I still haven't taught my first class, and God only knows if I ever will. That's bad enough, but the rest of the classes are closed, too. That's over a hundred children! And nobody seems to care. You would think that Samara Orunbayeva would care. She loves the school. But she doesn't seem very upset. They've all forgotten about the school and are running around trying to earn money. It's like someone's put a curse on them. What kind of culture is this?" she wondered as she watched the sun disappear behind the mountains.

Then Erika remembered about Sovietbek. From the very outset, she had hoped that she would have a special relationship with this private man with sad eyes. Not exactly love or anything intimate, just pure friendship. That had been her initial thought. The longer she was there, the surer she became that if she ran into trouble she could count on Sovietbek above anyone else. But Erika had begun to have doubts after spending time with him herding and talking. She didn't know which direction their relationship had taken after that strange day.

"There's probably nothing between us. Definitely nothing," she thought to herself. Sovietbek had shown himself to be extremely odd. He had called himself a fascist and an *afganets*. Erika did not know what that last word meant.

She asked Samara Orunbayeva when she went home that evening. "Samra-apa, is Sovietbek not a Kyrgyz?"

"Why do you say that?" Samara Orunbayeva asked with a surprised smile.

"He said he is an *afganets*."

Samara Orunbayeva's face grew cold. "Why did he say that to you?" she asked, displeased.

"*Afganets* means another person, right?" Erika asked cautiously.

"It isn't something we should talk about, dear. That was during the war."

Next Erika wanted to find out why Sovietbek called himself a fascist. She knew what the word meant, but she did not know how it related to Sovietbek. She did not ask Samara Orunbayeva because she could tell that the subject was unpleasant for both mother and son. It was yet another unanswered question in the troubled soul of this foreign woman in Asia.

***

Eventually Erika came up with a courageous idea. She threw on her shorts and t-shirt and ran over to the boys who were watching the girls sunbathe from behind the trees. The boys drew their own conclusions about the sudden appearance of a teacher and ran off, but Erika quickly caught up with them.

"Do you want to study?" she shouted.

The boys stopped running. They were still smiling and red-faced from the recent sight of their teacher's nakedness and paid no attention to what she had just asked them.

She repeated the question again in a loud voice, "Do you want to study English?"

"Sure," they replied.

"Then come on: Hurry!"

The teacher's unexpected proposal fired up the mischievous boys, who were tired of doing nothing and were always up for pranks. They loped off behind Erika, picking up pieces of wire and metal along the way.

They had no difficulty breaking the old lock that hung on the school door, and soon a dozen boys were sitting at their desks looking up at their foreign teacher.

"This is my first class. I am very, very happy! You will call me Erika. Erika Klaus. I will ask you your names in English. I will remember your names quickly. Then we will be good friends. I love having you as my students. Very much."

***

Chet's next tragedy happened late one July night as the uncatchable cicadas chirped their loud, unending song. The monotonous sound, always coming from the same invisible point, made every living being within hearing distance, feel drowsy. The night watchmen at Bronza's Post were no exception.

Since many of them had learned to sleep deeply while standing to attention, it was the guard dogs who noticed the rustling sound first, and even they did not notice it immediately. The escapees were already a fair distance away and making their way confidently through the outskirts of the village when two fighting dogs broke loose from their handlers. The speed with which the escapees were moving aroused the dogs' predatory instinct.

The chase followed the river bed upstream, and then the dogs turned up into the foothills. When the escapees' footprints led towards a steep cliff lined with a smudge of dark bushes, the soldier in command shouted a hoarse command to the dogs. The dogs instantly picked up speed, overtaking each other as they ran. Soon the soldiers heard the dogs fighting with the unknown runners. There was no shouting or shooting, just the sound of angry growling and snarling. Soon all was quiet again. When the soldiers reached the scene, they found one of their dogs at the edge of the cliff whining and licking a cut on its leg.

The next morning, everyone in Chet with the exception of Erika, was shaken to learn of the night's tragedy, which they passed on to each other in secret: the Principal's brother Askarbek and his young bride Gulchakhra had fallen to their deaths from a cliff above the Chet River. A ferocious border post dog called Friendly had died with them.

Samara Orunbayeva forbade her daughters from mentioning the tragedy to Erika because she knew that Bronza was already extremely displeased that the girl had opened up the school and held her first class on her own. People assumed he was making up his mind what to do, but no one could guess what his decision would be. It was therefore best not to have anything to do with the foreign teacher, much less share news with her that, by rights, would result in information being sent to the Post.

In the meantime, despite numerous warnings from the Post, Erika had yet to provide it with information of any kind.

The Melon-Shaped Pillow

Occasionally Bronza was visited by ideas and schemes that were grandiose in comparison with the actual scale of Chet. This time his dreams turned to the completion of his bunker. According to Kagan's plan, in addition to being a reliable shelter from which he could command his forces during the bombing that would come in his war against his chosen enemies, the bunker would serve as a store for weapons and as a hiding place for the increasing volume of valuables, currency and drugs that made their way into his hands. For now, Bronza would use the bunker for peaceful purposes, which meant he would hold his "dangerous prisoners" there, girls who were trafficked, illegal migrants and terrorists selling weapons, until he personally decided what to do with them.

Lying in the sunroom on the roof of his house, Kagan wondered whether or not he should show his bunker to the powerful people he was closest to, in the countries he needed.

"Why not: On Border Guard Day I'll invite the President of this sheep -herding republic to pay a visit. He'll smell the greenbacks a mile away and come running. I'll hang a portrait of him in the bunker and hang the damn

Kyrgyz flag next to it. He'll be so happy he'll faint. But I wonder if he'll keep on being *khan*? I could help him as much he needs. That would make him crawl on his belly in front of me. Just look at what all the other *khans* are doing; they all plan to rule until the day they die. That's good for me, and it's good for them. I wish our old fart would do the same thing. Then at least I'd know who to pal up with and who to blow off.

"But that's not the main thing. My bunker provides the surest means of getting into Europe. They can't get enough of my girls and my goods in Europe. Lots of cities already have official drug bars open 24-hours a day. I must keep the dark-eyed girls and cellophane bags coming! Then I can use my sales to get through to the people in power in Europe. They hover like flies around everything I'm selling. The bastards just want to have a good time!"

Bronza turned over onto his stomach and put his melon-shaped pillow under his head. He was about to take a nap when the duty officer called to inform him that an emergency committee from the Kyrgyz Border Service had arrived.

"I'm not here! Tell them to fuck off!" Bronza replied, sharply accenting the end of each word. He remembered that *Marlenov*,[26] the head of the little republic's Border Service, had long wanted to cause him trouble.

"Ask them why they're here," he said into his radio.

"They say they're here to investigate complaints, sir!"

"Then they can definitely fuck off!"

A minute later Marlenov himself called Bronza on his satellite phone. "This is your last warning, Colonel! Disobeying orders will get you prosecuted under martial law. You're sitting in Kyrgyzstan, and don't forget it! I want you to open up this Post immediately for my people to investigate the complaints we've received. We have a whole pile of them. You won't be getting off this time, Colonel!"

Bronza made an effort to keep his voice calm. "This Post is operated by another country, my dear Minister."

"I am well aware of why your post is still here and what you've been up to for the past several years. Moscow may have forgotten about you, but we'll remind them. I'll drag your ass in front of a military tribunal, Colonel. Talking

26 *Marlenov – a combination of the names Marx and Lenin*

time is over!"

The Minister hung up. Bronza's neck went red and his straight, masculine lips tightened in a thin line.

"Asshole!" he hissed through his teeth.

The Goat

"Speak of the devil and he'll usually show up." The meaning of this Russian adage can often be observed in interpersonal relations. When Bronza finally found the nerve to place a direct call to the President of Kyrgyzstan, they had no sooner begun talking when their voices were united in a harmony of cooing that gave them both a great deal of pleasure.

"Ha, ha! Comrade Kagan! I hear that Kagan is more powerful than the President. Did you know that?" the President laughed. Then he promised to consider Bronza's invitation to attend the opening of a new residential facility for personnel at the border post.

A few days later, the President called Bronza back. This time the leader told him that he would be flying over several mountain villages to assess the damage caused by recent mudslides. He would end his trip by landing his helicopter at the Chet border post, but he could only stay for forty minutes.

The men understood each other perfectly. Bronza was grateful to the President for taking time out of his busy schedule leading the country to cook up a so-called "emergency trip" to come and visit him. That is how people treat their most trusted partners.

When the President arrived in Chet, the soldiers on the parade ground and the villagers around its perimeter were all dressed for a holiday and were waving the flags of Russia and Kyrgyzstan. Banners reading "We Guard the Fatherland's Borders with our Lives," "Long Live the Border Partnership between Russia and Kyrgyzstan," "Truth and Justice are our Guides," "Fight Bribery," and "The Land of our Fathers is Holy" were hung everywhere; in front of the Post headquarters and on the facades of buildings, dormitories, warehouses and the cafeteria.

The holiday decorations were topped off by smiling portraits of the two countries' Presidents beneath flags on silver flagpoles.

And, of course, Bronza's wind ensemble provided a military march tune appropriate to the occasion.

The VIP guest's first words were, "I see that this border post is well organized and running smoothly."

"I enjoy the effort, Mr. President!" Bronza replied with a salute and a click of his heels.

The President was expected to listen to a brief report by the head of the border post on the post's statistics for the year, but the written report recited by Bronza was so full of Soviet clichés and bombast, that the guest's attention soon wandered.

"Good job! I want to thank you for your excellent service in protecting our country's borders!" the President broke in approvingly.

Later that night the border post hosted a banquet in honor of the President. Everything was carried out in accordance with military etiquette. The key moment was to be the toast.

Bronza felt anxious as he stood with his glass at nose-level. He was trying to sense whether or not his guest was pleased by the banquet. The words the President spoke did not matter. What mattered was the look on his face, and his face did not look good. There was something metallic in his voice, and while his eyes stopped on almost every officer in the room, they avoided Bronza. The President seemed to be ignoring him, as if he wanted to demonstrate that the other officers were more worthy of his attention.

"Bastard," Bronza fumed inwardly. "Just watch him shit on all the presents I gave him. What about the snow leopard coat and the gold saber? Forget those. What about the million bucks he has right there in his wallet? It mustn't be enough for him. He's worked up one hell of an appetite since he became *khan*. What am I going to do? Give him more? I'll have to give him more. That scumbag obviously knows how I make my money and he might just decide not to renew my contract next year. He's capable of anything."

As the President was getting into his helicopter, Bronza finally saw what he wanted to see on the man's face: a pleased smile. Every fibre of Bronza's being was filled with resolve. Without hesitation, he grabbed the President in a bear hug, held him tight and said in a voice intoned with loyalty, "If it comes to it, I'll put all my chips on the table to ensure that you keep running the country."

Early the next morning, when the President awoke from a short nap in his helicopter, his assistant informed him that Marlenov from the Border Service had been shot in the night.

"Marlenov?" the President gasped. He did not believe his ears.

"One shot to the back of the head. Outside his house," the assistant added, fiddling with the holster around his waist.

The President sat up in his chair. Fear coursed through his body.

"He is supposed to be armed at all times," he said to nobody in particular. Then he whirled around to face his assistant, who stood behind him.

"Is he alive?"

"He died at the scene."

The helicopter leaned into a turn as it prepared to land. The rest of his military ministers were probably down there waiting for him.

"That makes six," the President thought. It was a frightening number. "In only six months."

He silently counted up how many of his ministers had been killed in the fight to divvy up the government's property. It scared him, but there was nothing he could do to stop the assassinations. He allowed each of them to have armed security teams paid for by the State. He provided all of them with cars with bullet-proof windows. Nevertheless, the killers kept finding them and his ministers fell, one by one, to bullet and knife.

Now it was Marlenov, an extremely cautious officer who was educated in Moscow. True, he had a sharp tongue, but he was committed to stability. On the other hand, the President's assistants had made him aware of what was going on in the Minister's private life, especially his relationship with his children and his brothers.

He thought back to what Bronza had said about Marlenov: "A great leader and a fine man." The words were still loud in his ears because he had heard them only forty minutes earlier.

In his heart, the President agreed with Bronza. "Yes, we have truly lost a good leader and a fine man."

THE EIGHTH STEP: CRUEL SUN

"The horses are very tired! They feel bad! Why hurt them?" Erika tried to stick up for the horses that the boys of Chet were racing back and forth across a field for fun. When they heard her, the boys sniggered. The foreign woman's naivety caught them off guard, but then they spurred their horses even harder. They were playing *ulak tartysh*.

From the sidelines it looked like football, except that the players were on horseback and instead of a ball they were dragging the headless body of a downy young goat. Each team was trying to throw the goat into the other team's goal. Goaded on by the riders' *kamchi*,[27] the horses struck croups in a fury, fell down, jumped back up with their teeth bared, and trampled the body of the goat kid, which was covered with dust and dirt. The players had to lean down out of their saddles, pick up the body, break out of the pack and race to throw it into the opposing team's goal. None of them managed to do it very often, and the feat was always accompanied by bruised faces, cut arms and legs, and sometimes bloody noses.

Erika couldn't bear to watch the terrible scrum of men and horses. As she sat among Chet's spectators, her heart ached and she didn't know who to turn to in protest against what she was watching on the field. Her eyes looked for Sovietbek in the crowd. Perhaps he was against this cruel Kyrgyz game, too? But he was not there.

Sovietbek was becoming more and more of a mystery to her. When he was home, he stalked around looking like an angry tomcat, and then he would disappear for days on end, without warning.

Erika put her hands over her face to avoid seeing what was happening. Just then, someone called her name. She turned around. It was Samara Orun-

27   *Kamchi – (Kyrgyz) a whip made of braided rawhide leather.*

bayeva.

"They want you down at the Post. Why didn't you go yesterday or the day before? You can't do that, sweetheart. I'm getting in trouble because of you!"

"You're getting what?"

"Trouble. They want to punish me because of you. I'm the Curriculum Director and you live with me. That means I'm responsible for you. Do you understand, sweetheart?"

"I don't want to go to the Post."

"What do you mean? You have to go! It's a government post, not a private company!"

"They want to make me an in-for-mer."

"That's fine. We're all informers. It's the only way. There are people breaking the rules everywhere you look. Spies and saboteurs. We have to help the Post, sweetheart. It's state business!"

"I don't want to informs."

"You have to inform, sweetheart. How else can they collect information? And they'll pay you for every piece of information you give them. The pay is pretty good these days."

"I don't know how to informs."

"We'll teach you, sweetheart. There's nothing to it. Now go down there today. If they give you an assistant's contract, just sign it! Do you understand?"

"It's you, I don't understand." Erika countered.

Samara Orunbayeva's voice rose to a shriek. "Don't you land both of us in trouble!"

Erika had always thought of Samara Orunbayeva as being kind and gentle. She had never seen her angry before. It was easy to see how this woman, who could go from sweet to furious and cold in an instant, was capable of leading an entire school. Erika did not want to make her any angrier, so she adopted a more respectful tone of voice.

"It is extremely bad to informs, Samara-apa."

"Stop saying 'informs.' You're supposed to say 'inform.' And there's nothing bad about it. Just take the paper and write down what you see and hear. Or call them. They'll give you a number where you can call them.

Erika respected Samara Orunbayeva, but she realized that there was no way for the conversation to remain polite. Without another word, she went into her room and locked the door.

"We didn't invite you here to teach us how to live!" Samara Orunbayeva called through the door. Then she left the house.

"I bet they'll try to do something to me now," Erika thought. She was lonely and unhappy. Everything in the room seemed strange to her: the bed she was sitting on, the table and chair, the lamp. She was afraid, but at the same time, somewhere deep inside, her alter ego protested against everything that was happening in Chet.

***

The village administration had one policeman on its payroll. The title on his contract was "neighborhood policeman." The skinny young man, a bachelor, hated his blue police uniform with its three sergeant's bars on the shoulders and always changed into civilian clothes whenever he had the chance.

He had got the job after a period of unemployment because he knew the *akim* of Chet, but the older man had warned him, "It isn't an easy job. You'll get to know every troublemaker, thief and alcoholic in town."

There was little the policeman could do to suppress that kind of crowd because of his slight build and ignorance of the law, so he spent more time asking God to prevent fights than actually stopping fights or punishing the parties involved.

He was relieved to hear the akim's latest order. The man wanted him to find the foreign volunteer teacher, deliver a warrant for her arrest and take her to see the investigator at the Post.

"What's a warrant?" Erika asked.

"It's an order: Like a warning."

While the girl slowly read through the document, the neighborhood policeman, whose name was *Stalbek*,[28] eyed her curiously from head to toe. She was wearing shorts and a thin t-shirt. He had been officially informed that a single woman from far away in the West had come to Chet and that the *akim-*

28 *Stalbek – form of the name Stalin*

iat[29] was responsible for her safety while she was there. That meant that he, as neighborhood policeman, was personally responsible for her but Stalbek had not had the time to call Erika Klaus down to his office or visit her to make her acquaintance and provide the foreign subject with official instructions.

"I do not want this order," Erika said. She held the paper out.

"What do you mean you don't want it? It's an order from the Post. See? There's Bronza's signature."

"Who is Bronza?"

"He's the head of the Post."

The policeman did not take the paper, and Erika did not know what to do with it. She looked him in the face. His eyes did not seem angry or cruel.

"You have to go. Otherwise there will be difficulties."

"I really do not understand. Why do I have to go?"

"We're right by the border. It's military law here. Everybody has to obey the Post."

"Why does the school obey it?"

"The school has to obey, and so do I, even though I'm a policeman. I can't refuse an order from Kagan."

"What is Kagan?"

"Oh, you know. That's what folks call Bronza. It means the same thing as khan."

"Do you mean like Genghis Khan?" Erika asked.

Stalbek laughed. "Exactly: Genghis Khan. Bronza is our Genghis Khan."

"I don't want to see Genghis Khan!"

"It's the head of the Post who wants to see you, not Genghis Khan. I was just joking about Genghis Khan."

"I haven't done anything."

"But I have this order."

Erika looked into the policeman's kind eyes. They were begging her.

"Let's go," he invited her with a smile.

Erika decided that maybe she would go, but she certainly wouldn't sign any papers...

"Can you call Bishkek for me: to the Peace Corps?" Erika asked.

29 *Akimiat – local government*

"You have to do that from the Post. They have a special phone. We don't have any other way to contact Bishkek from here."

"Will you help me?"

"Sure."

***

The duty sergeant took Erika to the office of the investigator, Major Nigmatulin. The major squinted to see who was coming in.

"Oh! It's the lamb. Come on in, dear. I understand that you aren't used to things around here and you don't know the rules in the border zone. Am I right?"

The major stared at Erika as she sat down, but she had not understood the question.

"You are new here," he went on, "but you've already managed to work up a dossier with us."

Erika looked him straight in the face. "I don't understand."

"We have a dossier on you. I've already been working on it for a week. Why didn't you come to see me?"

"I am a volunteer. I teach children English. I 'm not interested in anything else."

"How clever of you. Then let's look at your dossier. You have the right to see it. Listen carefully, lamb. Our operatives accuse you, Erika Klaus, a citizen of the Kingdom of Norway, of coming to Kyrgyzstan's border with China under the pretence of volunteering while concealing the true reason for your trip. Secondly, you have been engaging in subversive behavior. Specifically, you encouraged the school students to break into the locked school and occupy it for purposes we have yet to ascertain. Thirdly, it says here: 'Erika Klaus and the local electrician Sovietbek have approached the border several times in order to study it.' My dear Erika Klaus, I demand in the name of the law "On the state borders of the Kyrgyz Republic" that you answer these charges. I have not made any of this up. This is what I get from my operatives. Do you understand?"

"I don't understand anything," Erika replied truthfully.

"I'm giving you a pen, some paper, and an empty office. You have unlimited time. Write the truth and only the truth. Otherwise you will drag yourself into a swamp. Is that clear?"

***

Late that evening they took Erika to see Bronza.

"What are you scuffling about for, ugly thing!" Bronza yelled as soon as Erika appeared in the doorway. It was an automatic response to the sight of the pale, unattractive girl. He showed his disgust without any reservation.

"You don't have to be friendly with us, but you will be in the beauty contest! That's my order!"

Bronza didn't look at Erika's dossier or talk to her. He pressed a button and told his assistant, an enormous young lieutenant: "Get her ready for the beauty contest!"

"Yes, sir! The beauty contest!"

The lieutenant beckoned for Erika to follow him. She had understood none of Bronza's words, so before she left she decided to voice her complaints to the head of the border post.

"I really do not understand why the school is closed. Why do you have a dossier on me? Why won't you give me my passport?"

"Go with the lieutenant, pretty girl. He'll tell you what to do. Now run along. There's a fine man waiting for you!" Bronza replied with a sneer.

Erika was shocked at such treatment. Her face flushed red, and then it paled. She wanted to protest, but the lieutenant was already pulling on her shoulder.

***

"Are you going to call the Peace Corps?" Stalbek asked Erika when he saw her in the hall.

"What Peace Corps are you talking about? She has to get ready for the beauty contest!" rumbled the lieutenant leading Erika.

"I really must call the Peace Corps!" Erika was almost screaming. She reached for Stalbek. He took her hand and looked up at the tall lieutenant.

"She needs to call the Peace Corps."

"What the hell is that?" the lieutenant asked. Then he looked at Erika.

"It is my guide. I must call."

"I'm not the telephone operator, kid," the lieutenant answered haughtily. "Come on. I have to take you to headquarters. You can ask them for permission to call your guide."

***

The so-called "beauty contest" took place the next morning. The jury consisted of Bronza and two foreigners, who sat on a raised stage in the *Red Corner*.[30] One of the men represented the Sheikh of Bahrain. The other man was European. Both were travelling in the guise of businessmen.

Grouped three at a time, heavily made up girls taken from the jail for illegal migrants paraded in front of the men wearing nothing but bikinis. After making a few turns, each of them was supposed to take off her bikini top and say her name and age. If a buyer liked one of the girls, he wrote her name down on his list. The young girls tried to smile pleasantly and make eyes at the "jury". They were willing to go anywhere and do any kind of "work" to get away from the Post.

"Anybody still back there?" Bronza barked when the "beauty competition" drew to a close and his clients had each chosen seven or eight girls.

"Just the volunteer. But she won't come out, sir. She's biting. She doesn't want to do it."

Bronza turned to his clients. "Let's go. We'll look at her back there."

"Now this isn't to everybody's taste," he announced cheerfully as he presented Erika. She was in solitary confinement with her hands tied behind her back. "You may not like her, but the Sheikh might take to the wolf cub."

The Sheikh's representative hurriedly excused himself in broken English. "His Majesty warned me that he is only interested in beautiful girls. His harem

---

30 *Red Corner – the Soviet name for the club room at each military installation where soldiers were exposed to propaganda.*

is the best in all the islands of Bahrain."

"Sure thing," Bronza agreed with him. "But the Sheikh needs servants, doesn't he? You have already turned down three of my girls, and this makes four. Why don't you take them for two thousand each? They'll come in handy."

Erika really did look like a wolf cub. Her eyes glittered blue with anger. She had obviously been crying, biting her arms, beating her head against the wall and scratching her face until it bled.

Bronza looked at the European with one eyebrow raised. The man studied Erika for a minute, but then he turned away.

"Unfortunately I'm just a broker, not a dealer. I can't make that decision by myself, so I'll make enquiries. By the way, Mr. Bronza, how did she end up here?"

"My dear friend, you can run into anybody anywhere these days. They're all out there, trying to get lucky."

"I see, Mr. Bronza. When will the helicopters be here?"

"Tonight at twenty-four hundred hours. Be ready to go. We'll pack the lambs for you. The helicopter will take you to your flight from Tashkent to Vienna through Istanbul. The papers are all in order. For God's sake, don't fuck up at Customs. Our boys are everywhere, so don't go to the wrong ones."

Suddenly they heard Erika's strong voice from the back of the cell. "I need a helicopter!"

"See? The girl wants to go! Take her!" Bronza stared at the European broker.

"How much do you want for her?"

"She's cheap. You got the others for forty thousand a piece. I'll take a lot less for this one. Thirty. Shake!"

Bronza held out his hand, but the broker backed away. "No thanks. I was just asking. I couldn't pay for her just now, anyway. If we decide to buy her, I'll let you know right away."

"Fine: See you later!"

***

"You're a government employee. You have the right to tell anyone to…" Stalbek tried to assuage his anxiety has he stood in Bronza's reception room. The sergeant's nerves were on edge. The colonel was an army officer, and in this country army officers were upper class government employees, while the police were definitely lower class. Even so, the sergeant had resolved that he would do all he could to fight the colonel, the head of the border post. He was confident that he would prevail, but it was taking Bronza a worryingly long time to see him. He'd already been in the reception room for a solid hour. He was pretty sure that everyone at the Post had already been in to see Bronza. Officers, ensigns and sergeants entered Kagan's office one after another and came out with varying grimaces on their faces, but even though Bronza knew Stalbek was waiting he did not call him in. Finally the policeman lost patience.

Stalbek opened the door after the last visitor had left and Bronza was alone. "Allow me to come in, sir!" he said, his voice trembling.

"Oh my, the head cop is here to see me!" Bronza snorted, his red eyes bulging.

"Sir," Stalbek began, but his voice stumbled. He was extremely agitated. "I will have to file a report with the Peace Corps about what has happened to Erika Klaus here."

"What are you talking about, boss?"

"You had her arrested illegally and you're keeping her in the slammer. She is under the protection of the Peace Corps, sir."

"Who?"

"The school volunteer Erika Klaus."

"I mean what is the Peace Corps?"

"It's…" the sergeant began to stutter. He was not sure what the Peace Corps was. All he knew was that the *Akim* had told him the Peace Corps protected foreign volunteers.

Seeing that the policeman was stalling, Bronza jumped in to make fun of him. "The Peace Corps is me!" he roared, pointing at his chest. "Didn't you know that? Almost the whole West does business with me these days. I already have Russia in my pocket. In case you're interested, all the presidents need me. All of them want to have secret little talks with Mr. Bronza. Because

Bronza is powerful and famous. His fame precedes him! You should know that, sergeant! You ought to know what the Peace Corps is."

"It's an organization," Stalbek finally answered.

"Screw them, whoever they are! I'm talking about something else. You have to be able to see through people, both morally and physically. All people are cowards by nature." Bronza adjusted his holster. "And right there in that skinny chest of yours, brave policeman, is the soul of a rabbit. All of you people have to be managed, commanded and directed like a bunch of blind men. I'll take cities and entire countries, or better yet, I'll take their fat-belly bosses and use them to get at the neo-fascists, or skinheads, or flying Dutchmen, whatever they're called. Then I'll be able to turn the world upside down: Especially with the help of those buggers in the 'Slavic brotherhood.' That's what I'm talking about!"

Bronza bent down and took a picture out of his desk to show to Stalbek.

"Do you recognize this man?"

"Yes."

"Who is he?"

"Bin Laden."

"Is he an astronaut?"

"No. He's a terrorist."

"I'm going to be meeting him soon."

"What are you saying? You'll be arrested, sir!"

"Not if you don't turn me in."

"Me?"

Stalbek lost his nerve completely. He didn't know what to say to the colonel. He was still confused by all the absurd and boastful things Bronza had said that seemed to have nothing to do with him. At the same time, the policeman was surprised that Kagan was sharing all this with him. Was it all a plot? Was the colonel intentionally trying to scare him? Or was it just simple paranoia? What was he supposed to make of Bronza's threatening announcement that he would be meeting with the terrorist all the police were looking for?

The sergeant was so shocked by the unexpected revelations from Kagan, who was imposing and usually off-limits, that he momentarily forgot why he had come.

"Have you ever heard the expression *memento mori?*" Bronza asked abruptly, his eyes drilling into the policeman.

"No." Stalbek sounded cowed.

"It means 'remember death.' Death is always near. It's always following you: Right on your heels. Did you know that?"

The sergeant was not able to digest everything in this extremely odd conversation with the head of the border post, so instead of answering he looked up briefly and then lowered his eyes.

"Dismissed!" the colonel commanded.

Just then the policeman remembered why he had come. Sounding indecisive, he asked, "What about the volunteer? What will happen to her?"

"Nobody bought the little bitch. I'm deciding what to do with her. Want me to give her to you as your wife? If you take her, I'll let her live."

Again, Stalbek was struck dumb. His blood rushed to his face.

"But she's a volunteer," he spluttered.

"Who the fuck cares? Volunteers are always looking to get laid. So take her. For free. You can work off the debt when I give you a special assignment."

Stalbek rose unsteadily from his chair, saluted weakly and turned towards the door. A minute later he returned to Bronza and bravelyannounced; "Give her to me. I'll take her!"

Bronza laughed. "Remember, if you let her leave Chet you're a dead man. My men will go to hell to find you if they have to. And keep your trap shut. Got it?"

"Yes, sir."

"And from now on, you will be answerable to the Rules of the Charter. Understand?"

"Yes, sir! Sir, will you let her use the special phone to call Bishkek?"

"Who?"

"The volunteer."

"Not a chance, Mr. Cop. We've got serious charges against her. She refuses to work with the Post. When everything's going smoothly maybe I'll let her call. Just so you know, you are now responsible for her behavior. She'll be your faithful wife, after all." He chuckled.

"Can I take her home, sir?"

"Go ahead. Just remember everything I told you. And fuck her as much as you can. It'll make her sweeter. The little bitch bites like a mad dog."

"Yes, sir. Will the school re-open?"

"I'm going to have dogs search it first. Then I'll open it. What do you want with the school?"

"Some of the parents are complaining, sir."

"Tell the bastards to fuck off!"

THE NINTH STEP: ALIEN SUN

Erika looked at the sun through the bars on her window. Today the sun seemed cruel and cold. It was not the same light the people of Chet had taught her to worship. Today she had no desire to hold her face to the sun, close her eyes, fold her arms over her chest and bow three times while repeating the words of the ancient Kyrgyz sun incantation she had memorized:

Oh kind, benevolent Sun!
Rise clear and gentle above the earth!
Show the lost traveler his way!
Warm the sick and the cold with your rays,
Do not hold back your living energy,
Give warmth to the plants and beasts
And send people your joyous light
Oh kind, benevolent Sun!
Sweep the pitiless threat from us.
Chase the pitch black away.

Now Erika felt that the sun was alien and hard. It made her want to break off forever, the threads of hot, loving feelings she had always harboured for the sky god. The sun seemed to welcome the protest coming from the heart of a tiny, far-off little girl on earth whose emotions had been tortured. It even seemed to laugh at her. Whenever it came out from behind a cloud, the girl saw its ironic, gloating face. Thus the sun swam through the grey sky, casting an unconcerned glance from time to time at the child who had loved it the day before.

Erika turned away from the window. The indistinct, distant thought of suicide she had borne for the past day suddenly sprung up in her head as a real desire. She began looking around at the objects in her cell. There was a metal bed and mattress. A bedside table, a cup of water, a stool and a fold-out table attached to the wall…

***

When evening fell, the bar across Erika's door was slid back and the policeman Stalbek was let in.

"Please excuse me," The sergeant looked haggard.

Erika did not even hear what he said. She looked at the person standing in front of her with indifference and then lowered her eyes. The sergeant saw that she was devoid of any desire to express her anxiety or anger. He did not know what to do next.

After hesitating, he repeated, "Please excuse me."

Erika remained silent, so he continued. "I didn't know that they would behave like this or I would never have followed their orders. But maybe things would have been worse if I hadn't brought you in. I think they are capable of anything."

When he had finished, Stalbek realized that nothing he had said had registered with Erika.

"Let's go," he said, and bent down to take her hand. "I will take you home."

Suddenly Erika shuddered and pulled her hand away. She glared at him.

"I will take you home. Or you can come to my house. Kagan gave me permission."

When she heard the name Kagan, Erika raised her head. "Kagan is truly criminal," she said. She began to come to. "We have to call the police."

"I'm a policeman and I'm standing right here. But nobody can do anything to him."

"Or you?"

"I am a little person: Just a sergeant."

Erika's head dropped. She was thinking.

"We have to call the top police," she said, looking up at him.

"They're all tied with the same rope."

Erika's face was strange. "Rope? Do you have rope?"

"What do you want rope for?"

"Just get me some rope."

Stalbek became suspicious. He was a policeman, after all. "She wants to hang herself," he thought.

"Let's go. I'll take you home or wherever you want. To Samara Orunba-yeva, or to my place?"

"I won't go with you!

It's Samara-apa I want to see. I want to tell her everything."

The Afghan Girl

The Kyrgyz of Afghanistan, who, for over a century, had borne much sor-row because of the Post in Chet, thought for a long time. They needed to decide who in Chet they could trust to carry out their holy act of justice and revenge.

They had decided on the act together, at a large gathering where they sac-rificed a white mare and prayed to Allah with their hands in the air, reaching out to Tengri.

"May the all-powerful Uluk-Allah punish anyone who breaks this sacred oath. May the children in his line be born monsters for seven generations, and may their descendants always bear the mark of the outcast!"

When the time came to choose a person from Chet, everyone at the gathering knew that they would hear the name of Sovietbek. And they were right.

"He is a direct descendant of the Tsaritsa of Alai, *Kurmanjan Datka*.[31] He saw the death and suffering of the Afghan War first-hand. He knows how Soviet soldiers tortured the local people. And the Soviet court martial condemned him to death by firing squad because he tried to protect an Afghan girl. But Allah supported the cause of justice. A bomb hit the trench where the judges were, and they all died before they could execute Sovietbek."

"People say he ran away from the war."

"Who? Sovietbek?"

"Yes."

"I haven't heard that."

"Let's not worry about whether he ran or not. We have other business to discuss. Will he agree to command our unit?"

"I think he'll do it gladly. They say that their Kagan Bronza is planning to get rid of Sovietbek soon."

The Post

When the Soviet Union's soldiers left Afghanistan, the local nomadic Kyrgyz tribes took control of a BTR-60 armed personnel carrier and a ZIL truck that had been abandoned in the mountains. They hid them for years in the forest, covering them with the branches of bushes. Then, with the help of Taliban fighters hiding out with the Kyrgyz, they repaired them and used them to haul cargo. Now they decided to use their arsenal against Bronza, or rather, against the evil Post that had stood for over a century between two fragments of the same small, unlucky people.

When he heard of their plan, Sovietbek, who was sitting cross-legged on the ground in a damp cave, dropped his head and covered his face with his hands. He was shocked by this insane, desperate plan which his dispossessed brothers had cooked up. They hoped that their "military force" would be able

---

31 *Kurmanjan Datka – 19th century ruler of the Alai region in Kyrgyzstan, called the "Tsaritsa of Alai" by the Russian Empire. The Kyrgyz of Afghanistan and the people of Chet are direct descendants of the legendary Kurmanjan Datka.*

to put an end to one hundred years of suffering.

"Where is your carrier?" Sovietbek asked in a hollow voice.

The faces of the three Kyrgyz, seated in front of him in the cave, were radiant. Appointed by the council of the Kyrgyz of Afghanistan, this was their first meeting with Sovietbek, a man considered a legendary hero by their people. In their naïve fantasies, Sovietbek was like Manas from the legendary Kyrgyz epoch, renowned for killing countless enemies and uniting all of his brothers as one force.

"It's there, not far from the Post."

"What do you mean, not far?" Sovietbek raised his head in surprise.

"In Chet. In the *Aksakal's* yard."

"At the *Aksakal's*?" Sovietbek became animated.

"Yes, *Oktyabr*."[32]

"Okay. So how did you get it there?"

"We made up a contract so it would look like Oktyabr bought the carrier from us. Then we legally brought it through the checkpoint. We paid them in gold bricks."

"Where's the truck?"

"We have it at home for now."

Although Sovietbek had initially felt overwhelmed by this naïve plan of his inexperienced brothers, he found himself admiring them for the amazing feat they had accomplished. Given the harsh regime in effect at the Chet border post and in the village, who would ever have expected a surprise like this? It was unthinkable! But then he remembered something that made him fearful about the outcome if this crazy plan were put in motion by Oktyabr and the Kyrgyz of Afghanistan. He was sure that someone from the village had already informed the Post. After all, Bronza paid handsomely for that sort of thing. But why hadn't the Post done anything yet? That was the strange thing.

"How long has Oktyabr had the carrier?" he asked.

"A week."

Concealing his astonishment and concern to avoid frightening them, Sovietbek continued with his questions

"Does it have a machine gun?"

---

32   Oktyabr – named for the October revolution.

"Of course."

"Bullets?"

"One full round."

"That's it?"

"Yes, but we can buy more. They're easy to buy near at the border."

"Now tell me how you plan to take the Post with one BTR."

The men glanced at each other. Then the oldest of them answered, "That's hard for us to say. We are not military men. I suppose you'd have to use the machine gun to shoot all the bastards at the Post and then blow up the main building. Our people have chosen you as their leader. You know better…"

"Me? You chose me as your leader without even asking me?"

"We all count on you, Sovietbek-baike. Don't let us down. We are all descendents of Kurmanjan Datka, aren't we? We are your brothers."

"Yes, my brothers, we are kin." Sovietbek cut them off. He did not want to hear this keening of his Afghan brothers. It hurt him to hear this request from his simple kinsmen, who, like children, had no idea what they were asking him to do.

Sovietbek looked piercingly at his visitors. "We don't have to shoot all of them. And we don't have to blow up the main building. One man is in charge of everything there."

The faces of the three men fell, and their reaction was sharp.

"You don't want to kill them?"

"It's not just one man!"

"They're all murderers, Sovietbek-baike. We counted up how many of us Kyrgyz Afghans they've killed. It works out to be three times one thousand."

"Three thousand?"

"Or more. But we can't be sure how many of our people they've killed over the one hundred years we've been trying to cross the border.

"The border post in Chet was built by the Russian Empire. Since then they've done a lot of evil. We can't find all the guilty parties now. We need to think about who the criminals are today."

"Why bother thinking?" one of the men cried out, staring wide-eyed at Sovietbek.

"If we don't think it through, we'll all end up dead. And for no good reason. The Post has enough arms and ammo for a third world war. I want you to get rid of that BTR right now. Otherwise they'll find out and a lot of people will get hurt because of it."

The oldest of the three bristled. "What about the Post?"

"Let me think about it. I'm the commander."

The men were too upset to say anything.

Rope

That morning eagles were flying through the valleys and foothills as was their habit, looking to add variety to their diet. Instead of mountain sheep and ulars, they were hunting for rabbits, groundhogs and other small animals. The eagles flew slowly in even bands, planning their movements carefully so that they could study every inch of the wide valleys.

Most of the birds were grown-up youngsters. The young eagles often fell out of formation, and from time to time they played like children, dive-bombing crows and magpies. Always nervous, their targets skittered from bush to bush, pursued by the eagles' broad wings and sharp eyes. The outing was a chance for the young birds to learn to hunt and live on their own.

There were many small animals living in the Chet valley, but the young eagles were rarely successful at catching any of them. Each animal of prey had its own means of escaping their deadly claws. Indeed, the prey was so expert at slipping away in the nick of time that the inexperienced eagles were often in danger of hitting the ground too hard. Even more experienced adults some-times ended up with injuries. For example, when rabbits sensed the enemy in the air, they froze next to a rock or a cliff, only to dart away or leap up at the last minute so that the attacker collided with a rock. One veteran rabbit flipped onto its back at the last moment and hit its enemy with its powerful hind legs.

Groundhogs and gophers saved themselves by diving into the nearest hole or under a bush, so adult eagles had to use their skills to try and chase them out into the open for the young eagles to catch, but even this approach was sometimes dangerous for the eagles. Every creature had its own way of fighting to save its life.

Bronza turned to Sovietbek. "How long are they going to fly around in the valleys?" They were making their way uphill to the high crags where the eagles had their nests. Both men were equipped for climbing, with ropes, crampons, climbing hooks, knives and pick hammers in their packs. They also wore Tricouni boots. Unlike Sovietbek, Bronza carried a pistol under his arm.

"Not for long. Usually an hour or an hour and a half," Sovietbek answered. He was in front, acting as guide.

"Do you think we'll get to their nests before they come back?"

"I think so. And we'll have time to set out our nets."

They were both breathing hard because of the altitude. It's true: there's no escaping fate. The two men harboured a deep-seated hatred for each other, yet they found themselves held by the same rope as they climbed together, each of them contemplating the best way to carry out his plan.

It all began when Bronza expressed a desire to catch an eagle in its nest and drink its fresh blood while standing on the top of Alatoo. This idea had been suggested to him by his deceased friend Mergen. Bronza had been eating snakes for several years on Mergen's advice, and now he decided to vary his elixir with eagle blood. He had to have the best guide from among the local hunters to take him up the cliff.

"Take the *afganets*. He doesn't drink or smoke, and he teaches all the local hunters," Major Sidorov told him.

When he heard this, Bronza gazed at his deputy for a while without saying anything. His eyes were guarded. He said nothing on the subject until the next day.

"I guess that's a good idea. Bring him to me!" he ordered. Secretly, though, he was not sure that it was such a good idea to take Sovietbek. First of all, he was a veteran who had served in a bloody war. Secondly, the *afganets* had probably suffered a concussion, even if he chose to conceal the fact. All of those vets had head injuries. And most importantly, whenever Sovietbek had to look Bronza in the face, there was something wolfish in his eyes. Why was that? Bronza had pondered about this on more than one occasion when the *afganets* came to mind, but he could find no answer. Since he had no answer, he would have to get rid of the man before he caused trouble. It was a good idea to stay ahead of events.

That was Bronza's philosophy, but for some reason he had not yet got rid of Sovietbek. The climbing trip seemed like a convenient excuse. He would have to be careful that nobody associated him with the messy business, but he figured it wouldn't be hard for him, a hardened "tiger" of the border service, to knock off the lousy guide after grabbing the eagle from its nest. One shove and the body would go over the cliff to where no bones would ever be found.

"An accident," Bronza thought with pleasure. His lips curled in a sneer.

***

Stalbek warily made his way toward Samara Orunbayeva's home. He had two tasks to carry out. The first was to convey Bronza's order to Sovietbek. He also wanted to at least catch a glimpse of Erika. The need to see her had slowly taken hold of him, growing from the moment he first saw her. By convincing her to go to the Post that first time, he had unwittingly harmed the girl, who had trusted him. After experiencing all that torture and humiliation , Erika had even wanted to hang herself. It was a good thing that Samara Orunbayeva ran down to the Post at the last minute and talked Erika into going home.

Because of the stress she had endured, Erika spent an entire week in bed, unable to stand. Samara Orunbayeva's whole family cared for her, especially the two daughters. On Stalbek's frequent visits to see Erika, his face betrayed his shame. When Aichurek and Saikal heard how their volunteer had been humiliated at the Post, they directed their childish hate against the homely policeman. They considered him to be a traitor and an enemy. The girls refused to accept the jars of jam and juice Stalbek brought for Erika, and told her about it.

She approved of the refusal, saying, "You did the right thing."

Stalbek stood at the door of Sovietbek's house, dressed in his policeman's uniform and afraid to knock. He planned to wait until someone came out of the house. There were strange people milling around in the yard. Because they were illegal immigrants and refugees and he was a policeman, they looked at him with hostile eyes. He was their number one enemy. Stalbek knew he was supposed to check the documents of these people who had appeared in Chet from out of nowhere, but he didn't have the courage to do so. He knew that everything these people did , and everything that happened around him , was done with Kagan's permission He decided he was better off standing with his back to the suspicious individuals as if they were none of his business, so that's what he did.

Suddenly he heard Sovietbek's voice right behind him:"Hi there, Sergeant!" Stalbek spun around. "Hi."

"Are you here to see Erika again? Why don't you leave her alone?"

"No. I'm here to see you. Kagan wants you!"

"Who?"

"You!"

When he realized that the policeman wasn't joking, Sovietbek was immediately on his guard. Had Kagan got wind of something? It was impossible. Stalbek hadn't done anything about the conspiracy of the Afghan Kyrgyz yet, and he hadn't told anyone about it. The three men who had come to him had returned immediately to their home across the border. A plan had been maturing in Sovietbek's mind ever since then. It was still in the formative stages, and still inside his head, so he decided to pry the policeman. Perhaps he knew why Bronza wanted to see him.

"What does Kagan want with a handyman? Don't they have their own electrician?" He waited to see what the policeman would say.

Stalbek, however, had turned his thoughts to his own affairs as soon as he had delivered Bronza's message. He was thinking about Erika. If she heard people talking, she might come out of the house. Just out of curiosity. Or she might come out of the house on her own business. But Erika did not appear. It was time for him to go back to the Post and report to Bronza that the message had been delivered.

"Are you deaf or something?" Sovietbek asked rudely.

"What?"

"I asked you what Bronza wants with me?"

"I don't know. Ask him! Maybe he wants to take Erika from me and make her your wife."

"What the fuck?"

"He gave her to me. To be my wife."

"Who?"

"Erika."

"Bronza did?"

"Who the hell do you think?"

"That's bullshit. She's a foreigner. She's under the protection of the Peace Corps. They don't understand that kind of shit."

"What can the Peace Corps do? They won't drive their tanks up here. And even if they did, that bastard would blow them to pieces. You know that as well as I do."

"The hell I do. Forget it. What time do I need to be there?"

"You're already late."

Sovietbek wavered for a minute. Then he decided to risk it and go and see Kagan. Otherwise he'd have to go and hide out in the hills, and that didn't fit into his plans at the moment.

Seeing that Sovietbek intended to go to the Post, Stalbek thought there was no need for him to go, too.

"I'll sit here by your house until you get back," he said cunningly.

Preoccupied by his thoughts about the imminent meeting, which would probably contain an element of conspiracy, Sovietbek nodded and left.

***

When he got to the Post, the first person to meet him was Major Sidorov, not Bronza. When the Major explained what they wanted, Sovietbek grew even more apprehensive.

"Kagan's up to no good," he thought. He wasn't sure what to do.

"Can I think about it?" he asked the Major.

"What is there to think about? It's not the first time you've gone!"

"Yeah, but even so…" Sovietbek mumbled, thinking hard. "Just give me an hour to think. How was I supposed to know you'd ask me to guide Kagan himself?"

"I'd be happy to do it, if I were you."

"That's true, sir, but…"

Suddenly Sovietbek had an idea. He'd do it. When the thought came to him, his face changed and went pale. The Major did not notice. He was just glad he had managed to convince the stubborn *afganets*, even though he knew his boss didn't care much for the man.

"Make it an opportunity. Do the boss a good turn and you won't be sorry. You know how generous he can be," the Major added. He slapped Sovietbek on the shoulder.

***

The seemingly endless, silent kingdom of mountain peaks rising high above the glaciers was full of life. The mountains are ruled by two forces of nature, the sun's rays and the winds which, working together over the course of centuries had polished and shaved the tectonic rock, changing the configuration and even the great height of the cliffs and peaks.

A little lower, under the cover of snow and ice, was a third force of nature: life-giving water and moisture. Here there was plant life, ranging from moss and wild onion to juniper bushes. This, in turn, provided food and cover for the few animals living among the peaks: jerboas, snowcocks, wild sheep and mountain goats. And reigning over them all were the eagles, the kings of the blue sky,

Two men, Bronza and Sovietbek, made their way towards the eagles. Each of them secretly hated the other. They were joined by the same rope, a rope that could bring death to either of them. Sovietbek walked ahead as the guide. At just the right moment he could let go of the rope Bronza which held onto. If he did, Bronza would lose his balance and fall like a rock. But on the other hand, Bronza could pull hard on the rope to make the same thing happen to his guide. Both men were counting on this as the easiest way to fake an acci-

dent, but their plans differed slightly.

"I'll do it after we go down under the cliff, when we're on our way back from grabbing the eagle," Bronza decided. He gazed at the taut safety belts crossing Sovietbek's back.

The higher the cliff faces became as they climbed in their Tricounis, using pick axes to aid their ascent, the faster Sovietbek's heart beat. He had to get rid of Bronza here, before they reached the eagles' nests, or he knew he might be too late. He felt as if Bronza, that sly old fox, was reading his mind as Bonza climbed behind him, preparing to do something to stop Sovietbek.

But he did not want to be a cowardly killer. He wanted to mete out a just punishment to the despot, the man who kept apart two branches of the same kin, and he wanted the man to understand what the righteous punishment was for. Sovietbek wanted to turn around and scream in Bronza's face everything that ought to be said at the very end: "This is for you, Bronza, and your damned Post: For the blood and sorrow of thousands of my brothers, for the defiled honour of hundreds of my sisters and mothers! This is for all the filthy crimes committed in Chet, for turning the people of my village into shameful informers and depriving them of their humanity. For all of this, my hands will mete out death to you and the rest of your fascist scum!"

Then Sovietbek would be able to look the man in the eye with a clear conscience before he shoved him in the chest.

Just then, Bronza let out a yell. "Don't let go of the rope, you son of a bitch!"

Sovietbek had absentmindedly let the rope go slack in his hands, and without thinking he pulled it hard to keep a hold on Bronza, who had begun to lose his balance. When he looked back, he saw that Bronza was hanging on the edge of a steep drop, gripping the rope with both hands. Sovietbek's hands were all that held him. After a dazed second, Sovietbek opened his hands. Then after fumbling for another few seconds, he managed to unhook the rope from its spike. In that instant, however, Bronza managed to press his chest against the massive granite and grab at its flaky surface with the tips of his fingers. His legs hung in the empty air. With just the right effort, his right leg could grasp a protruding rock. A sense of deadly danger shot through Sovietbek. Instinctively, he rushed over to Bronza, who was grappling for his life. When the man reached out his hand, Sovietbek kicked his shoulder.

There was a short cry and Bronza's body, twisting in the air, disappeared beyond the cliff into the deep valley.

***

After standing there for a few minutes, feeling empty and not knowing which way to turn, Sovietbek suddenly saw a few flakes of snow whirling in the air in front of him. They were followed by a harsh, cold wind that slammed into his body, still trembling from the stress. It was the beginning of one of the snowstorms the area was known for. He had to find cover. He had no sooner made his way around the cliff from which Bronza had fallen, when Sovietbek suddenly heard several pistol shots fired in rapid succession. His heart froze. It was Bronza! He was signaling to his men!

THE TENTH STEP: MERCIFUL SUN.

Once the Sun had become a cold stranger to Erika, she did not see its face again for a long time. It remained distant and glowering for many days. It took all the spiritual warmth of the people around Erika to bring the Sun back to her. There were many people around her now: the schoolteachers, Samara Orunbayeva's family and, most importantly, her students. The street-wise children of Chet already knew that their English teacher had wanted to hang herself while she was at the Post, and because they knew, they looked at her with complicated, mixed emotions. Some of them felt sorry for the unfortunate foreigner. Others were surprised to see that even a pale little girl could find the strength to end her own life. There had been suicides in Chet, but always for very serious reasons, so serious that the dead had been buried away from the village cemetery. No *khanaza*[33] had been performed, and people

---

33   *Khanaza – Muslim prayer over the dead.*

quickly forgot about them.

And then, all of a sudden, the girl who had come from so far away to teach the local children had tried to put a rope around her neck! One of the older students even mentioned it when he wrote his next information letter to the Post. He had obviously not taken into consideration that the event took place at the Post, so there was no reaction to his letter.

By the next day, almost everyone in Chet knew that Kagan had given Erika to the neighborhood policeman to be his wife.

"Our Kagan is so wise! That was a just decision," the elderly members of Chet society intoned in delight. "Who else would ever marry the poor man? He'd die a bachelor."

The young people, even though they were from and of Chet, turned out to be more in favour of such concepts as love, mutual acceptance and such like.

"Let's see what the newlyweds do," they said, and prepared themselves to wait.

"The groom's walking around like nothing's changed."

"It must be nonesense about Kagan giving them to each other to marry."

"It isn't. People heard the story directly from Kagan."

"Then he'll make them get married."

"Or he'll stomp all over them himself."

"The hell he will. He's got plenty of pretty girls up there."

"If they disobey Kagan it'll be lights-out for both of them."

"Yeah, right. He's got more important things to do."

While people were discussing her, Erika remained oblivious to all the rumours and gossip and slowly began to feel like herself again.

"Will you be going to class tomorrow?" Samara Orunbayeva asked her before bed each evening. At first Erika only nodded. Then she began to say "yes."

Finally she said, "I'm now more than happy to return to my class

At last, after many days, Erika prepared to go to sit on Sovietbek's "sun throne" behind the barn. Aichurek and Saikal had been constantly begging her to come with them. Both girls had been studying with her at home and were starting to write and, even better, speak English.

"You are my very best students. I love you very much," Erika told them. It made her happy to see Samara Orunbayeva's daughters doing well.

"Will we work on our English today?" Aichurek asked.

"Excellent. Let's get on with it!"

Dressed in shorts and t-shirts, the girls opened the door to go outside.

"Stop!" Samara Orunbayeva cried. "There are Muslims out there in the yard. They'll beat you up for looking like that. Put on something decent."

Erika was surprised. "You're also Muslims."

"We aren't that kind of Muslims. And they're Afghans and Arabs. Their sharia laws keep women from even showing their faces to strangers."

The girls put on long dresses, but they did not bother with headscarves.

"Put on your sun hats," Samara Orunbayeva said sternly.

When the girls went out into the yard they saw a small cluster of bearded men wearing skull caps. They were standing around Stalbek and arguing about something. One of them grabbed Stalbek by his collar and tried to drag the policeman into his hut. Stalbek struggled to get away. It was obvious that the "illegal immigrants" felt much more confident than the member of local law enforcement.

Once the girls were behind the barn the arguing got quieter.

"Will they kill the policeman?" Erika asked the girls.

They shrugged, at a loss, and began to remove their dresses. When they were in their underwear, they lay down on the sunbed. Erika sat down next to them, her shoulders hunched.

"Maybe they've already killed him," she said without turning round.

"That's not true," Aichurek spoke up. Saikal said nothing, but she studied Erika's worried face with a curious smile.

The girls got comfortable on their backs and took up the pose their volunteer had taught them. Hands behind their backs and eyes closed, they took slow, even breaths. They lay like that for half an hour without saying anything. This was their time for deep thinking and dreaming under the kind, familiar Sun.

The Sun seemed soft and gentle to Erika that day. The bright globe looked tenderly down on Erika, carefully, so as not to distress her already wounded soul. The Sun God truly felt pity for its own, tiny little piece of humanity: Erika Klaus.

Erika collected her thoughts and tried to focus on what was most import-ant, but she was unable to do so. Only now did she begin to realize that her heart had suffered so much sorrow, protest, anger, despair, disappointment and hate over the past few days that it had no room for happy daydreams about how she would see her mother and father in Oslo in a year's time.

Erika lay still and taut. She could not focus on any one thing. Everything in her head was jumbled up like the colours and patterns of a kaleidoscope. Out of this chaotic riot of thoughts came a sharp shot of worry: what had happened to the policeman when he had been surrounded by all those men? Was he alright? Was he even alive?

***

Erika's intuition was right. The bearded men beat Stalbek senseless be-cause he had supposedly been watching them for days, even though Kagan had given them permission to be in Chet.

Stalbek was in a bad shape when he got to the clinic at the Post. For three days he lay suspended between death and life.

When he finally emerged from a coma, he whispered, "It's not her fault."

The orderly in the clinic guessed who the poor policeman was worried about and laughed. "Would you listen to this? He thinks he's Don Juan."

"He's just worried about his lawful wife."

"The boss was just poking fun at him, but the dumb ass took it seriously."

"Hold on. If the boss said he'd marry them, then he'll do it. He'll make her marry him."

"The bitch won't do it, and the dog won't jump her. She's a foreigner."

"What do you know about it, fool? And when did you ever see the boss divide people into foreigners and non-foreigners? He doesn't give a shit who people are or where they're from!"

The Uniform

Bronza began to appreciate his miraculous rescue as he lay in the hospital room in his bunker, with his head on a woman's lap. He had not lost consciousness as he fell from the cliff, but for several moments he lost his tongue.

During the whole dreadful event, while he was hanging from the climbing rope with its end fortuitously jammed between two rocks on the cliff face, while the special operatives pulled him up to their helicopter, and while travelling back to the Post, Bronza had not uttered a word. His eyes were huge in his deathly pale face, and his thin, dry lips trembled slightly. His nostrils were tense and the tip of his pug nose was even whiter than his face.

His underlings, from Major Sidorov to the helicopter navigator, were terrified by their daunting commander's silence. For one reason or another they all felt somehow guilty for what had happened to their boss. They hadn't taken care of him!

For understandable reasons, Major Sidorov was most afraid; his whole being shook with fear and he wrote himself off as a dead man.

At the same time, Sidorov couldn't help but wonder who had caused the accident. Could it really have been the *afganets* he had recommended as a guide? Or had something else happened? Maybe the Colonel had tripped and wouldn't blame anyone for the accident. Hoping to get some information, any information, out of him Major Sidorov tried to question him once they had got Bronza, into the helicopter: "That really turned out well. Can I ask you what happened, sir?"

Bronza ignored the question. It was obvious that he hadn't heard his deputy's words. After that, no one dared disturb the Colonel. Even his personal physician decided it would be best not to try to talk to him.

As soon as the sentries stationed at high points around the Post had informed Major Sidorov that shots had been fired in the valley, he immediately ordered a search party to find the eagle hunters. They had saved the head of the Post, but the other man had disappeared into thin air. There were no tracks or signs of him, so once Bronza was back at the bunker Major Sidorov personally took charge of the search for the *afganets*. All day, a military helicopter hung low over the high peaks where only eagles wheeled and turned.

***

By two-thirty, Bronza seemed to snap out of his shock. He was still lying in bed with his head on the lap of his favorite woman, Alyona.

"I heard a voice," he whispered furtively.

At first the woman said nothing and kept stroking his cold forehead. Then she decided it was a good thing he was finally talking.

"I've been lying here all day and wondering whose voice it was. At first I thought that it was me who was yelling when I fell off the cliff. That's what I really thought. But it's impossible. I would have recognized my own voice, wouldn't I? Then I thought that maybe it was thunder. But there's never thunder in July. Then I finally realized that it was The Voice."

"I don't understand, dear. What Voice are you talking about?"

"A voice from above. He saved me."

"Do you mean a voice saved you?"

"Yes."

"Do you mean God?"

"Exactly!"

"Interesting…"

"That's exactly it. The Creator chose me again. He chose me for something big. Now I get it. If he saved me so miraculously… From now on I'll do everything my God tells me to do: With all my heart. Everything I've done up until now was right, Alyonushka! I'll never leave you."

"You promise?" Alevtina laughed insecurely.

"I'll leave the rest of them, but I'll never leave you. Bring me my hookah so we can have a smoke."

"Some people have been pressing me to give you a message. For three days now some big people have been waiting to see you, but I don't want you to get up. They can wait a little longer."

"Who are they? Get my assistant in here!"

Alyona threw up her hands. "Here we go again." She went out to call the assistant.

The Captain clicked into the room wearing the new khaki uniform Bronza had instituted and saluted by putting his right hand to his chest with his elbow out.

"Captain Chalov has arrived, sir!"

"Who's out there waiting for me?"

"They won't say, sir. They're both foreigners. One says he's a General. The other says he's a Mullah."

"I'll see them tomorrow morning."

"Yes, sir! Tomorrow morning!"

When the Captain left, Alyona exclaimed, "Your boys' uniforms look pretty good: Absolutely gorgeous!"

"It'll take a while to teach these idiots my new trappings. What do you think? Do I look good in the new uniform?"

"Of course you do: Especially in the General's uniform! It looks like it was made for you. I swear you look like a Marshal in it!"

"Hold on! But you're right. The Commander needs to be a Marshal. That day isn't far off. First the 300 Committee[34] has to issue its first order. Followed by a second. And then everything will fall into place.

"I'll need a high rank for my international projects. That General out there is one of Russia's top skinheads. And he's head of Russia's National Security Council. I have to at least be on his level when I talk to him. We've got important decisions to make. I'm talking about billions of dollars. Now, that other guy out there is no Mullah. I've been expecting him. He's the top dog in Al-Quaeda. Do you know what that is?"

Alyona shook her head. "Uh-uh." Her eyes had lit up though, when he mentioned billions.

"It's a good thing, too. You don't need to know."

"I need to always be with you. That's all I need," she said and lowered her full breasts onto Bronza's naked chest.

***

---

34 *300 Committee — international group of leaders intent on making humanity serve the elite.*

The Snake *Ordo*[35]

Within one day, the Kyrgyz of Afghanistan had all gathered together in a narrow gorge at the large yurt of Asrankul, whom they had elected their khan. The last meeting of its kind had been the previous year, when they had received a reply from the Foreign Minister of Kyrgyzstan in response to their request to return home. When the reply was read out, Asrankul was secretly pleased, although he hid the fact. The others all cried like babies, especially the women. They wept loudly, scratching their faces and smearing the blood on their dresses.

"That damned Minister has a mother who is just like us! May her son die, so that bitter tears blind her eyes!"

"May the wretch never see his children again!"

The men, dressed in greasy old padded jackets and leather boots, their faces wrinkled and chapped by the wind, sat with their heads down and silently swallowed the tears that rose in their throats. There was no one to pity or console them. Khan Asrankul kept his head down. His mind was not on the Minister's reply. He was thinking about how to retain his position over his pathetic subjects and extract more out of them.

Now the Kyrgyz of Afghanistan were gathered again in the central gorge outside Khan Asrankul's big yurt, and again all of them were weeping. Only this time, the tears were tears of joy.

The day before, the American Freedom Radio broadcast had announced that the last Soviet leader of the former Chet border post between Kyrgyzstan and Afghanistan had died as the result of a climbing accident.

The announcer added, "This report is confirmed by an Astrol satellite photograph."

"Allah has finally opened the road for us to return home," croaked the father of young Gulchakhra, who had died the year before in Chet. He was old and ailing, but his neighbours had taken him to the meeting in a truck. The *Aksakal*[36] was supposed to speak holy words about Freedom and Home to his gathered kin.

---

35 *Ordo – (Kyrgyz) cave*
36 *Aksakal – (Kyrgyz) honored elder*

And he spoke. Standing in the back of a truck with his hand on the side, in a wavering, hoarse voice he spoke briefly, for he knew he could not last long. Even so, he overestimated his strength. Before he could say the last words, the very words everyone so longed to hear, his breath became so short that all he could do was lift his arms in a grand wave ;a final gesture that almost caused him to fall off the truck. This was his last speech to his people.

He had already considered himself dead after Gulchakhra, his only daughter, had been killed. When she died, he sat alone in his yurt, where he refused to speak to anyone. He kept the lights turned off, even at night, and never lit the fire. But whenever people walked past his yurt, they could sense that the old man was still alive. So they left bread and water at his door.

The Aksakal was surprised when the men came to tell him that he would have to give a speech at a meeting of all Kyrgyz. The old man sat for many long hours wondering if he had heard them correctly. Or was it a dream? How could it be? He was essentially dead, and here they wanted him to give a speech.

When the crowd repeated his words back to him ,shouting:"Home! Freedom!" the Aksakal became flustered, as if he were hearing the words for the first time.

The people decided that their Aksakal had nothing else to say, so they grew noisier. "Our commander Sovietbek has killed that damned Kagan! He did!"

"Soon he'll come and tell us all about it!"

"He'll get us official permission to return home."

"Now all he has to do is destroy the Post."

"It's already as good as gone. The shaitan[37] was all that kept the Post together!"

"I heard that Moscow ordered the Post to be closed a long time ago!"

"Yeah, but people will say anything…"

Suddenly Gulchakhra's father turned around and spoke again. "Allah has turned his face to us. We'd better get ready to move, my children."

Khan Asrankul shot him an angry look and turned away. He had hated the old man ever since he had refused to give him Gulchakhra as his wife when

37 Shaitan – (Arabic) devil

she was nine years old.

When evening fell, the people wandered back to their yurts still rejoicing, in order to pack up their meager, nomadic households and wait for an announcement of when they were to move.

"Put off all your *toi*[38] and other celebrations until after the move, when we are home," the Aksakal told them. Then he asked some young *dzhigits*[39] to take him back to his lonely yurt.

***

Sovietbek's heart was pounding and the pistol shots still rang in his ears as he leapt across the top of the mountain and raced into a short stand of junipers on the other side. Branches snagged at his elbows and the pack on his back. The motion would be visible to border soldiers with binoculars, even from a distance. In the first few minutes, his fear of Bronza, who was somehow still alive, was so strong that he did not even consider how, in his panicked flight, he was snapping the juniper branches. A short while later he froze like a statue.

A thought occurred to him. "What if it wasn't Bronza shooting? But then who? The only people in this area are guards with automatic rifles. So it was Bronza. Judging by the sound it was his TT. How could he still be alive? From that height? What am I going to do now? That bastard will go to hell to find me if he has to! That's the end of my plan. I really fucked up. I should have found another way to knock him off."

Sovietbek's first hot, tangled thoughts gradually began to cool off and he decided to sit where he was until night fell.

***

Detailed knowledge of the mountain paths helped Sovietbek avoid the eyes of patrolling guards and the noses of their dogs.

By the time the sun came up, he was already at the border with China, where he stopped a few hundred metres away from a border crossing. Good

---

38 *Toi — (Kyrgyz) wedding*
39 *Dzhigit — (Turkic) brave young man*

friends of his from the Post worked there. They would be able to let him get around the crossing through a secret tunnel. He needed to hurry to his friends as fast as he could. It was already getting light, and soon he would be in danger of getting caught. The search party could already have sent its own soldiers to the crossing.

But for some reason Sovietbek moved slowly. At first he did not understand the reason for his indecisiveness. Finally it came to him: at this very instant he could save himself from his pursuers, cross the border and disappear into the sea of Chinese, where nobody would ever be able to find him. The very thought made him angry. He began to sweat. His trembling fingers undid the buttons at his collar. He realized that his whole being was protesting against the idea of flight. He was about to run away like a coward after having made a mess of his people's cause and the cause he had always assumed gave meaning to his life as a man and a patriot : the fight for freedom and justice. What would he be worth if he ran?

Sovietbek took a few steps back and sat down under a bush. He could no longer see the border crossing or the rosy morning sky where the sun, Sovietbek's protector and god, would soon appear.

For a while he sat still, feeling empty. His anger at himself began to morph, turning into something decisive, something brave and definitely very risky.

Suddenly he remembered that the snake ordo was nearby. That was it! He could see the hole. He would wait here until Bronza came to get snake blood. Then he would finish him off. That would be better than living out the rest of his life as a measly coward.

Sovietbek looked toward the snake ordo and, his heart and nerves tingling, imagined that Bronza was there, his eyes bulging out and a pistol in his hand. No, Bronza was no fool! He would have to be careful, crawling up behind him so that he could kill him before the man knew what hit him. That was the only way to get him!

But wait. Would he come for snake blood? And if he did come; when? Sovietbek began to doubt his plan but tried to assure himself : "He'll come! I know he'll come! He didn't get to drink the eagle blood, so he'll be here tomorrow. His depression will drive him here."

***

After three days of anxious waiting in the underbrush, Sovietbek had to go down to the crossing point and ask his friends for bread and tins of meat.

The Sergeant on night duty was so startled to see Sovietbek that his eyes goggled.."What are you doing here? We have orders to arrest you!"

"Bronza?" Sovietbek asked.

"Who else?"

"Then arrest me," Sovietbek answered, forcing a smile.

The Sergeant fumbled for a minute and then rushed into his shack. He came straight back. "Listen, my friend, you'd better give yourself up. It'll be simpler that way. I don't know what they're hunting you for, but you'd better turn yourself in anyway. They'll go easier on you."

"This is all bullshit. The Colonel won't touch me. He loves me. You know that."

"I suggest you better turn yourself in before he leaves."

"He's leaving?"

"Yeah. I heard he's flying out tomorrow to get medical treatment."

"What time?"

"Who knows? But you'd better hurry up."

"I will! Thanks for the advice. Now give me some rations. I haven't eaten in two days."

The Sergeant ducked into his quarters and came back with a sack. "Here. Now beat it. Otherwise, we're screwed. Don't tell anyone you were here."

"Of course not! See you."

When Sovietbek raced into the bushes, bent low with sack in hand, for a split second, his figure was illuminated by the beam of a far-off floodlight.

THE ELEVENTH STEP: STRANGE SUN

The people of Chet were shocked by the news: their neighborhood policeman, that pathetic Stalbek, had actually taken the foreign volunteer home
with him to live!

"How did he do it? Drag her?"

"Kagan's orders."

"I know it was Kagan's orders. But what about the girl?"

"She must have obeyed."

"Try disobeying him sometime."

"It's strange."

"Nothing strange about it: They say he's pleased as can be."

"Who? Kagan?"

"Use your brain. The cop!"

"What about her?"

"They say she's happy."

"They must be screwing already!"

"What the hell else are they going to do? Play hide and seek?"

"That's one lucky fool."

"He's not an idiot. He's got a brain in his head. I bet he'll beat the hell out
of here with her. You and I are the idiots , sitting here in this shit hole without
a clue about what's going on in the world."

"What's going on in the world?"

"Anything you want, fool! Half of Kyrgyzia's already left. Life is on the
outside!"

"To hell with them: At least we have bread here!"

"That's for sure. You'll go and inform on me tomorrow and then have
plenty of bread."

"And you'll make plenty of bread from me in the same way, so shut your
fucking trap."

"Fine: Now let's finish this bottle and crawl home."

"Not so fast, sucker. Have you forgotten that you owe me another bottle?"

The Propeller

Sovietbek lay in the thick undergrowth of the narrow Chet valley right beside the path that flanked the helipad. The frost that had formed on his thick eyebrows overnight began to melt and drip into his eyes. He periodically had to rub them with his fist to keep them from closing. As long as the helicopter was there he knew that Bronza was at home. That meant he would come out soon.

The thought that he had proved himself incompetent in front of his enemy was very upsetting to Sovietbek. He was a man on a mission to reunite his people, and he would put an end to the years of groveling at the bastard's feet, even if it cost him his life. Allah would help him. Allah would take his soul into heaven. Truth and justice were on his side! The main thing was to seize the right moment to leap out and strike a lightning-fast blow with his knife to the devil's heart. Sovietbek was confident that he would succeed. Nobody, not the bodyguards, the officers, nor even Bronza, could imagine that he was waiting there. He was sure that he had the element of surprise on his side. As it got lighter around him, he crouched closer to the ground, like a predator preparing to spring its prey.

Sovietbek's eyes instinctively concentrated on his right, looking in the direction of the Post, from which he expected people to approach the helicopter. Suddenly there was a clattering sound on his left. Sovietbek had been so focused on the Post that he had forgotten about the helicopter, and his whole body jerked.

It took another twenty minutes for people to start coming out of the main building of the Post, where there was a secret door into the Bunker. Bronza was in a fine mood, holding hands with Alevtina and smiling at the people around them. He was followed by Major Sidorov, who did not look as if he had been punished for the accident at the eagles' nests.

As he walked behind Bronza, the Major leaned over to his Commander and listened to his instructions. All of them could see the helicopter up ahead, its noisy motor warming up. The wind from its propeller pounded everything in the area. When the people reached the wind zone, they bend forward and used their hands to keep the dust and sand out of their faces.

Sovietbek had not dreamed that he would have such a convenient opening, and he immediately leapt out of the bushes, knife in hand. The wind hit him in the face and kept him from making a precise strike at Bronza, who stumbled backwards. There was also a bodyguard whose enormous frame was shielding the Colonel from the wind. Stepping around him, Sovietbek lashed out with his knife, but it did not reach its target. The bodyguard behind Bronza then managed to knock the knife from Sovietbek's hand.

There was a brief tussle during which Sovietbek only managed to hit two sergeants before finding himself on the ground, held in place by soldiers' boots.

"You dirty bastard!" Bronza's woman screamed. Then she took off her shoe and hit Sovietbek in the face several times with its spiked heel.

Major Sidorov and the others stared in silence at their newly-minted "Commander-in-Chief", awaiting his orders.

Bronza turned to Sidorov. "I want you to deal with him personally before I get back. Show him no pity! And I want him alive!"

"Yes, sir. I will deal with him personally!" the Major replied, holding his right fist to his chest.

Raw Meat

After seeing his Commander off for a ten-day course of treatment abroad, Major Sidorov was in an angry and ambivalent mood. After his brush with death, Bronza had been so sneaky and rude around the Major that Sidorov did not know what to think. Would the boss punish him or not? And it was almost time for his promotion to Lieutenant Colonel. Would he get the promotion or not? He did know one thing: while Bronza was gone, he had put another officer in charge of the Post, even though according to rank, that job was supposed to fall to Sidorov, who was his first deputy. That fact alone told Sidorov he was in for trouble, especially after the attack that morning!

And now the *afganets* was behaving like an idiot, stubbornly keeping his mouth shut when the Major questioned him. Finally Sidorov decided to take a friendlier approach.

"I was the one who recommended you to be his guide, so you can tell me. What happened to the boss up there? You're the only witness! Let's hear the story!"

Sovietbek was sitting on the floor, handcuffed to a water pipe. By his face it was obvious that he had completely given up on life. The Kyrgyz of Afghanistan had been fighting for a century to be reunited with their brothers, and the shameful end to the fight was morally fatal to Sovietbek. He blamed himself more than anyone else. He was sure that his stupid defeat had ended everything. Lost hope disappears forever, and Sovietbek set his own, shameful period at the end of a story that had been so important to the entire Kyrgyz people. There was nothing in the world left for him to live for.

"Talk!" Major Sidorov barked angrily, but he got no reaction from the prisoner. Then he shrugged his shoulders and left Sovietbek with one of the "turds" who had been specially trained to beat confessions out of prisoners.

Without using any special techniques or methods, the turd beat Sovietbek with a rubber club. The prisoner barely reacted. The beating was repeated the next day. The turd didn't ask his client any questions. All he did was beat him, silently and methodically. He beat his whole body, from head to foot, working slowly.

After several sessions with the turd, Sovietbek's body was one continuous bloody bruise, like a piece of raw meat ready for the frying pan. The turd was sure that even a light touch would make his prisoner scream in pain, but to his surprise Sovietbek proved him wrong. The prisoner lay silent, like a dead man, but he was still breathing.

This meant that they would have to move on to the next procedure. The turd should have got Major Sidorov's approval since there was a chance that the client would die, but he had noticed that the Major was indifferent to this particular client, so decided to act on his own. If it worked, he'd get praised!

First he prepared a needle. Then he rolled off Sovietbek's shirt, tied a rubber leash around his biceps and stuck the needle into his vein with a sure hand. The plunger pushed the clear liquid from the needle into the vein, and the turd pulled the needle out. Sovietbek fell on his back and froze. After a while his body went into a seizure. It happened twice more before his tortured body began to convulse. His pupils dilated and his eyes rolled back in his head. Sovietbek's head shook and fell to one side. Spit came bubbling out of his mouth.

The turd was pleased. His client looked ready, so he whispered in his ear, "How did you get here? I asked you: How did you get here?"

The intravenous injection of scopolamine was supposed to make the prisoner talkative. It was a proven method that never failed. But Sovietbek remained silent. His eyes looked more alive and he seemed to understand the questions, but he kept his lips sealed by pure willpower.

The turd went for Major Sidorov, who decided to try interrogating the prisoner again.

"Do you know who Bronza is?" he asked Sovietbek, this time taking an oblique approach. "Who is Bronza? You know him well, don't you? Answer me."

Sovietbek's eyes lit up and then went dead again. His lips tightened.

"What other methods do you have?" Major Sidorov called to the turd.

"Scopolamine is the last step, sir!"

"I don't want to hear that! Use your stupid head and think of something before tomorrow!"

"Yes, sir! I'll think of something before tomorrow."

"And I want him alive, you bastard!"

"Yes, sir. I'll keep him alive."

***

By the next morning, Sovietbek was gone. He lay lifeless, both hands gripping his head as if in pain.

THE TWELFTH STEP: ANGRY SUN

Major Sidorov was terrified when he found out that the *afganets* was dead. Not believing his ears, he ran into the cell where the body was and froze.

"Damn it! Where is that asshole!" he yelled to the duty officers, meaning the turd. They brought the private to him.

"I told you to keep him alive, you son of a bitch!"

All of a sudden he imagined how Bronza would soon be yelling at him in exactly the same way. His order had been to keep the *afganets* alive. Major Sidorov could not understand why Bronza wanted the man who tried to assassinate him kept alive until his return, but an order is an order!

"Take this turd and let the other turds punish him!" he commanded the duty officers. Then he ordered the body of the *afganets* to be placed in the morgue, which consisted of two industrial refrigerators and an extra guard. He sensed that the body might disappear before the Commander-in-Chief got back. That would mean death for the Major. If that happened, the Commander could then accuse him of anything, even of being in league with the *afganets*. For the same reason, he refused to let Samara Orunbayeva take the body for burial. He did not tell her why.

When she went to the local Mullah and asked him to demand the body, the Mullah spoke sharply to her. "Samara-hanum, your son cannot be buried in the Muslim cemetery in Chet."

Samara Orunbayeva's heart went cold. "Why not?" Her drawn, grey face twisted in pain.

"Because it was his intention to kill a man. Sharia does not allow murderers to be buried alongside good Muslims."

"But he didn't kill anyone!"

"He wanted to kill Kagan. Maybe if he'd tried to kill someone else, but not Kagan…"

"What's the difference? He didn't kill anyone!"

The Mullah left the sorrowful woman without an answer.

Everyone at Samara Orunbayeva's house was in deep mourning. She and her daughters Saikal and Aichurek cried for days and nights, sitting with their faces to the corners of the room, with black kerchiefs on their heads. The behaviour of their neighbours and family made their position even worse. Afraid of the Post, and especially of Kagan, people did not visit Samara Orunbayeva to share her grief, as was the custom. Only Erika came, accompanied by Stalbek. He was risking everything he had, including his job and any future promotion. He was also afraid of running into the illegal immigrants in Samara Orunbayeva's yard. Despite all of this, the Sergeant stuck close to Erika. He followed her into the room where Sovietbek's mother and sisters were crying in the corners. Erika joined them, embracing her students and crying along with them. She had respected Sovietbek more than anyone in Chet. Even though he never shared his secrets with her, Erika guessed that he had some very important, very just ideas in his heart. She had once tried talking to him.

"Why are you so sad?" she had asked, looking at him with sympathetic eyes.

"I was born this way," he said, joking.

"Are you afraid I'll submit written information about you?"

"That you'll inform on me? :No, I'm not afraid of that."

"Then why don't you tell me the truth? I want to help you."

"You're already helping me."

"How?"

"You're teaching my sisters English. For free."

"And that helps you?"

"Of course. My sisters will grow up to be educated people."

"The girls are very good. And very pretty: Especially Saikal who is extremely beautiful!"

Erika had quickly realized that it would be useless to try to get Sovietbek's secret out of him, so she switched to talking about the girls. That was their last conversation. After that she saw Sovietbek only once more, when he stopped by to congratulate her and Stalbek on their wedding.

"We aren't husband and wife yet. But we are considering it," Erika laughed and blushed.

"You have to get married. You love each other."

Erika looked at Stalbek and laughed again. He put his arm around her shoulder.

"We don't even know how to kiss yet."

"You'll learn as you go along. You'll learn it all! Of course you will!" Sovietbek said with a meaningful smile.

And now he was gone. The disappearance of Sovietbek seemed inconceivable to Erika, a lie. Only the bitter tears of his whole family told her that the loss was real.

"Let's go together and ask for his body," she said to Samara Orunbayeva.

"It's no use!" the mother said. She began to weep again, swaying from side to side.

"How can this be happening? It's all so wrong. We must sue Bronza. Sovietbek was absolutely right. Bronza is a criminal!"

When they heard the foreigner utter these dangerous words, the weeping women fell silent. The policeman fidgeted in his chair.

"Sovietbek was a very honest person," Erika answered their silence.

Samara Orunbayeva sniffled. "Erika, daughter, be careful..." She put her handkerchief to her eyes.

Heavy silence descended once more on the room. Not knowing what to do next, Erika looked to Stalbek. He nodded as if to say, "Let's go home."

Erika replied aloud to Stalbek's nod. "Samara-apa is in a very bad way. So are Saikal and Aichurek." Stalbek said nothing and kept his eyes down. They sat like that a little longer. Then Samara Orunbayeva turned to the policeman with a question.

"We have family in Bishkek. Do you think we can let them know about my son's death?"

"Of course. Give me their addresses and telephone numbers."

"Will anything happen to them if they come here?" Samara Orunbayeva asked.

Stalbek was intent on helping the family of his friend, but this threw him off guard. "I don't know," he said and sat down again.

"They killed Sovietbek. What worse things can happen?" Erika butted in.

"It all depends on Kagan, and he's not here."

"He'll be back in a week," Stalbek told Samara Orunbayeva.

"People told me that he was going for medical treatment. But he went for a con-spir-a-cy. An international conspiracy." When Erika said this, the whole room quivered in fear. Another heavy silence fell.

"What international conspiracy?" Samara Orunbayeva asked, her voice trembling fearing the potential danger of the words.

"I don't know. Someone told me that."

"Who?"

"I can't give a name. She is my student."

Samara Orunbayeva looked at her daughters, just in case. Although they had heard the whole conversation, they still sat facing the wall. But they weren't crying anymore.

"We're going home to think about what to do next. If you need us, call." Stalbek stood up. Erika's careless words frightened him. Erika did not want to go with him, but he gave her a look that insisted she follow him.

The Rope Walker

On the night of the eighth day after the Commander-in-Chief's departure, the satellite phone suddenly rang at the Chet border post. It was Bronza. After talking briefly with the officer he had left in charge, he asked for Major Sidorov.

"What the hell's going on back there?" he boomed when the Major took the phone.

"Yes, sir, Colonel. I mean, Commander-in-Chief." The Major instantly corrected himself. "The *afganets* is dead. He was scared shitless and his heart gave out."

"I wanted to see that bastard alive. He was supposed to give me some information. Now I'll have to get the information out of you. But don't even think of running. You know I can reach any of you, no matter where you are. So you'd be better off thinking about the offer I made you. After what's happened you don't have any other choices. Or do you?"

Major Sidorov had not hoped for such a fortunate turn of events, so he blurted out his agreement.

"I don't have any other choices, Commander-in-Chief. I'll do it!"

"Good. You're not the fool I thought you were. You won't be sorry. You'll go after the top kills. Presidents, you know what I mean? And you'll make millions. But you'll always be on the side of justice, so you'll be clean in the eyes of God. Understand?"

"Yes, sir! Thank you, sir! Excuse me, sir, but what do I do with the murderer's body?"

"You've got a crematorium!"

"Yes, sir! The crematorium!"

Sidorov felt terrible when he hung up. Not long ago Bronza had asked him to join his team of hit men and he had refused. Now, while he knew that he had escaped taking a bullet over the *afganets*, it began to dawn on him that he had just agreed to be a hit man. Hired guns lived like rope walkers dangling over the pit of hell, and he had a beloved wife and children waiting for him back in Russia...

THE THIRTEENTH STEP: BLACK SUN

There were only a few days of school left. The short Chet summer was drawing to an end. The sun dipped low over the valley and it no longer seemed kind and gentle. Once again it became a cold stranger. Erika suffered from the change more anyone else. She felt that with each passing day ,she lost a little bit more of the thing that was dearest to her , the Sun. While the Sun was with her, her soul bloomed like a lotus flower and she was filled with a desire to help people, teach children and attain success. But most importantly, the Sun gave her a sense of fulfillment and love for people.

But what was happening to her now? The Sun was leaving, turning away, drying up, as if it had not been Erika's dearest friend just the other day.

Erika was in a bad mood as she walked to school. The dried grass crunched under her feet, filling her heart with sorrow.

Suddenly someone called her name. She turned and saw Stalbek. He ran up to her and grabbed her arm.

"Let's go home. We need to talk right away!"

"Why right away?"

"Hurry!"

Once they were in Stalbek's little room, he told her something shocking. "Someone has informed on you," he said breathlessly. "We have to run. They'll be here to arrest you any minute."

"Again! Who informed?"

"I don't know. The note listed everything you said about Bronza and Sovietbek at Samara Orunbayeva's house. That day they were crying."

"When we were crying?"

"Yes."

"When Sovietbek died?"

"Yes. Exactly!"

"But only the girls and their mother were there. There was no-one else."

"I can't tell you because I don't know. I guess they needed the money. But get your stuff together. We can still get through the crossing towards Bishkek with my police ID."

"Bishkek?" Erika was not prepared to run from Chet so unexpectedly. She stared at Stalbek in silence. It was hard for her to believe what he told her. She could never have imagined that Samara Orunbayeva and her daughters would betray her. She loved them with her whole heart.

"I don't have my passport," she said, trying to stall.

"I've got it. I bought it off one of the sergeants. Now let's go!"

***

Once upon a time, Bishkek was a city of nomads. For a long time you could still see the ruins of stone walls used to hold livestock, and of the mud huts which people lived in. But the city had grown quickly over the past one hundred and fifty years. Now it looks like an urban swathe of Central Asia, with noisy street bazaars and piles of fragrant melons.

"I will miss the melons a lot. They smell like the sun," said Erika, holding Stalbek by his little finger.

He was drenched with sweat from standing in a long queue in the stuffy airport, having managed to get her a transit ticket to London via Moscow.

"Here's your ticket," he showed Erika the green Aeroflot booklet. "I'm sending you back to Oslo to save you from the Post, but I want you to promise to be my wife after that. Okay?"

Erika smiled. "Okay. I'll invite you to Oslo." Then her face fell. "Stalbek, are you sure about it?"

"About what?"

"That Samara-apa, Saikal and Aichurek provided written information on me: Are you sure?"

"Why would I lie to you, Erika? I wanted you to stay in Chet and be my wife. It's a good thing the note went through a Sergeant who knows me. He showed it to me and told me that I had to bring you to the Post. I promised I would. I said I'd bring you there within the hour."

"Now Bronza will arrest you, Stalbek. Don't go back to Chet."

"He's not my boss. I'm a Government employee," Stalbek protested weakly.

"Don't go to Chet. Please, Stalbek! He is not scared of the Government."

Just then, the loudspeaker at Manas Airport announced boarding for the Bishkek-Moscow-London flight. People who had been snoozing on benches in the departure lounge began to move around, gathering their things together.

"It's time for us to kiss goodbye," Stalbek said, half-jokingly. Erika saw the tears in his eyes.

This time the kiss was long-awaited and desired on both sides. Standing away from the crowd, they hid in the shadow of a column and held each other tight, delighting in each other with their lips. Erika's whole body trembled and she moaned softly. Stalbek sensed that she wanted him. Extremely aroused, he momentarily forgot where they were and began to unbutton her shirt with shaking hands.

"We can't now," she whispered in his ear as she moved his hands away.

Blinded by passion, Stalbek again tried to kiss her and undo her buttons.

"But you're my wife!" he insisted, talking fast.

Erika was scared. She did not know how to stop him. "Yes, I am your wife. But this isn't allowed here!"

Stalbek was blinded by his fear of parting from this woman, the first real woman in his life with whom he had the right to sleep because she was his wife.

"Then stay here. I won't let you get on the plane!"

"We can't! I called Oslo. My parents are waiting for me!"

Just then the loudspeaker announced: "Would all passengers with tickets for the Bishkek-Moscow-London flight please proceed to the gate." The authoritative voice put a damper on Stalbek's ill-timed arousal. Seeing an opportunity, Erika quickly took his hands and crossed them on his chest.

When she spoke, her voice was sure. "Very soon I will call you to Oslo where you will be my husband. Okay?"

Stalbek was in no condition to think through everything he would have to do to go to Erika in Oslo; finding a ticket, flying to Moscow and then, God only knew how, finding his way to Oslo.

He wanted to possess his wife right there, at that very minute. He did not know what to say to her, so he said nothing, but his body was as tense as a red-hot crowbar.

Soon the long line of passengers stood outside ready to board the jumbo jet. Family and friends watched them through the glass walls of the airport. They were close enough for people to wave their last farewells. Erika and Stalbek did the same. Stalbek tried to put on a wide smile, pressing his face against the glass. He hoped Erika could see it.

Just then a woman wearing a red armband and hat went over to Erika and looked at her passport and ticket. Then she gestured for her to get into a white airport van that was parked nearby. When Erika got into the van, the door closed behind her and the van raced away down a service road. The whole thing took just a few seconds, and Stalbek didn't even have time to comprehend what had happened.

But he remembered Erika's lovely white calves, which peeked out at him so wonderfully, saucily, when she climbed into the van. The young man's body heeded the call, and the arousal that had begun to cool in him, returned in a wave of heat.

Then he came back to his senses. "Where have they taken Erika, my wife? What's going on?" For a brief instant he even imagined that she had been kidnapped by a gang of rapists.

He ran down to the first floor, to the door through which passengers departed for their planes, but the door was already locked. Then he remembered the airport police station and ran there. He found two cops playing chess. The others were asleep at their desks.

"Go and ask at Customs. Maybe they..." the captain told him, fiddling with his opponent's pawn that he had just taken.

The customs officers shrugged and said that as far as they knew, there were no problems with any of the passengers.

Stalbek ran back up to the second floor and saw a lonely blue and pink backpack, Erika's, sitting out on the concrete where the passengers had just embarked. The plane had already gone.

A thought screamed through Stalbek's head. "The Post!" The thought had been with him before Erika disappeared, but it had been dormant somewhere in his brain, awaiting its hour. Now it shone bright and clear.

"The Post had grabbed Erika! They had taken her to Bronza!" That was the worst thing that could happen to Erika and to him. Someone could be saved from any other place on earth, but not from the Post. It only obeyed the laws of the devil who ran it, and nobody could do anything against him.

Stalbek was a low-ranking cop and he felt that fact with his whole being. He remained standing at the glass wall, staring at the lonely backpack. His body and soul felt as if they were loaded with dynamite, but he still had one last hope. Maybe Erika would come back for her things. Then a man on a service motorcycle came and took the pack.

Stalbek stood there, alone...

***

According to the harsh laws of nature, eventually the young eagles' training on small animals came to an end. Today they returned to the valleys and
foothills, and once again there were more young eagles than adults.

It was autumn and the youngsters had grown, but they were still playful as
they wheeled over the Chet, glancing down from time to time with predatory
eyes at the village dogs, cats and chickens. But if one of them looked about to
attack, immediately a mother called out from above – xxx! – warning that the
village was dangerous.

A couple of their most experienced guides stayed high up right under
the clouds where they could see the whole area at once, wheeling slowly and
sending out signals to keep the rest of the convocation safe. Their sharp eyes
caught every suspicious motion on the ground and every irregular sound.

From high in the sky one of the eagles watched a man walking along a
deep ravine. It was hard going , the man sometimes slipped and sometimes
jumped from rock to rock, but he kept moving in the direction of the Post,
always keeping low to avoid being seen.

The man was Stalbek. He had made up his mind that Erika, his wife, had
been brought back to the Post. He would have to go carefully. He was sure
that the first border guard who saw him would arrest him. There must be an
order out for his arrest already. That much he knew for sure.

But, obeying the natural dictate of his heart, Stalbek put his goal of saving
Erika, at any cost, above whatever fear of death he felt.

                                    ✳✳✳

He was back in Chet by nightfall, to the one-room apartment he rented.
He did not turn on the light, feeling his way to where the key to his safe lay.
His service Makarov pistol and sixteen bullets were in the safe.

Finally, still moving in the dark, he drew close to his most important weapon, the weapon with which he could accomplish anything. He would free Erika
by shooting the guards at the Post, and he would even kill the terrible Bronza
, if he were able.

The hair on Stalbek's neck bristled. His right hand held the key and his left hand felt for the safe. It was not there. Then he decided that he was looking in the wrong place. He strode to the next corner, then the third, and then the last corner.

The safe was nowhere to be found! Stalbek froze. Was he in the wrong apartment? Horrified, he looked around. Where was his dagger? He kept it under the mattress of the torn couch he slept on. It was there! Stalbek grabbed it to make sure it was real. The handle of the steel dagger still had the smell of Erika on it.

When she had left the room for the last time, she held the dagger in her hand and asked, "Can I take this? To remember you by?"

"It's a real knife. They won't let you on the plane with it, and you'll miss your flight while they try to figure out where you got it from."

"I was joking," Erika twirled it in her hand and then put it back.

Gripping the dagger, Stalbek stood alone in the empty, dark room. His eyes were bloodshot. His heart pounded in his chest as it whispered an audacious plan: Erika, Erika…save Erika! What kind of nightmare is this? There's no way that I can escape my fate!

The End

Hertfordshire Press Title List

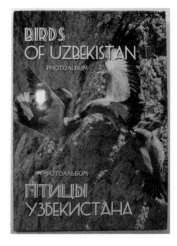

Birds of Uzbekistan

ПТИЦЫ
УЗБЕКИСТАНА

This is a superb collection of full-colour photographs provided by the members of Uzbekistan Society for the Protection of Birds, with text in both English and in Russian. Since the collapse of the Soviet Union and Uzbekistan's declaration of independence in 1991, unlike in other Central Asian states there have been no such illustrated books published about the birds of this country's rich and diverse wildlife.

There are more than 500 species of birds in Uzbekistan, with 32 included in the International Red Data Book. After independence, Uzbekistan began to attract the attention of foreign tourist companies, and particularly those specialising in ornithological tourism and birdwatching.

Birds of Uzbekistan is therefore a much-needed and timely portrait of this element of the country's remarkable wildlife.

RRP: £24.95

ISBN: 978-0955754913

When The Edelweiss Flowers Flourish
by Begenas Sartov

The author frequently explored the tension between Soviet technological progress, the political and social climates and Kyrgyz traditions in his work, and When The Edelweiss Flowers Flourish depicts an uneasy relationship between two worlds.
Using the science fiction genre, the novel's main character is Melis – derived from Marx, Engels, Lenin and Stalin – who has his counter in Silem, an alien being sent to earth to remove Edelweiss plants to help save his own planet from a deadly virus.
The essence of the story was attributed by Begenas to a childhood experience when a village elder helped him recuperate from breaking his arm, using a herbal mixture of seven grasses. These grasses – Edelweiss, Ermen, Ak kadol, Shyraajyn, Oo koroshyn, Kokomirin and Shybak – are still found in the high Kyrgyz mountains today, and are still widely used for their medicinal properties.

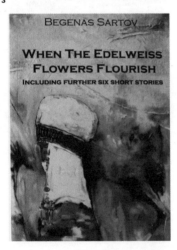

RRP:£12.95

ISBN: 978-0955754951

**Friendly Steppes: A Silk Road Journey
by Nick Rowan**

This is the chronicle of an extraordinary adventure that led Nick Rowan to some of the world's most incredible and hidden places. Intertwined with the magic of 2,000 years of Silk Road history, he recounts his experiences coupled with a remarkable realisation of just what an impact this trade route has had on our society as we know it today. Containing colourful stories, beautiful photography and vivid charac-

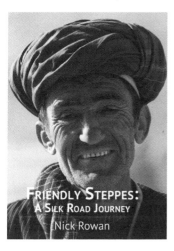

ters, and wrapped in the local myths and legends told by the people Nick met and who live along the route, this is both a travelogue and an education of a part of the world that has remained hidden for hundreds of years.
Friendly Steppes: A Silk Road Journey reveals just how rich the region was both culturally and economically and uncovers countless new friends as Nick travels from Venice through Eastern Europe, Iran, the ancient and modern Central Asia of places like Samarkand, Bishkek and Turkmenbashi, and on to China, along the Silk Roads of today.

RRP:£14.95

ISBN: 978-0-9557549-4-4

Under the Wolf nest: A Turkic Rhapsody
by Kairat Zakiryanov

Were the origins of Islam, Christianity and the legend of King Arthur all influenced by steppe nomads from Kazakhstan?

Ranging through thousands of years of history, and drawing on sources from Herodotus through to contemporary Kazakh and Russian research, the crucial role in the creation of modern civilisation played by the Turkic people is revealed in this detailed yet highly accessible work.

Professor Kairat Zakiryanov, President of the Kazakh Academy of Sport and Tourism, explains how generations of steppe nomads, including Genghis Khan, have helped shape the language, culture and populations of Asia, Europe, the Middle East and America through migrations taking place over millennia.

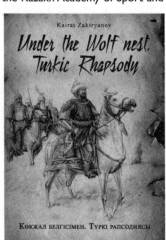

History is shaped by the victors, but after the collapse of the Soviet Union new attempts are being made to recover historical and ethnographical detail that previous empires swept aside. After reading Under the Sign of the Wolf: A Turkic Rhapsody you will look again at language and culture, and realise the living histories they represent.

RRP: £ 17.50

ISBN: 978-0957480728

Tales from Bush House
collected and edited by Hamid Ismailov,
Marie Gillespie, and Anna Aslanyan

This is a collection of short narratives about working lives, mostly real and comic, sometimes poignant or apocryphal, gifted to the editors by former and current BBC World Service employees. They are tales from inside Bush House – the home of the World Service since 1941 – escaping through its marble-clad walls at a time when its staff members began their departure to new premises in Portland Place.
In its collective authorship, it documents the cultural diversity of the World Service, showing how the extraordinary people who worked there, and the magnificent, chaotic building they shared, shaped one another. We use the word tales to signal that this is a book that mixes genres – ethnographic and folkloric stories, oral histories and jokes. Recounting tales involves an intricate relationship between talking and telling – as in the working life of a broadcaster.

RRP: £ 12.50

ISBN: 978-0-9557549-7-5

Igor Savitsky: Artist, Collector, Museum Founder
by Marinika Babanazarova

This is the biography of the astonishing life of Igor Savitsky, who rescued thousands of dissident artworks from Stalinist repression that survive today in the Karakalpakstan Museum, in Nukus, Uzbekistan; a collection of Soviet avant-garde art rivalled only by the Russian Museum in St Petersburg. The remoteness of the area, and its proximity to chemical weapons testing sites nearby, helped Savitsky keep his collection secret while, tragically, some of the Russian and Uzbek artists involved were either imprisoned or executed.
The author is the director of the museum, a post she has held since the death in 1984 of Savitsky, who was a regular visitor to her family. Savitsky's life is vividly narrated through detail from correspondence, official records, and family documents that have become available only recently, as well as the recollections of so many of those who knew this remarkable man.

RRP:£10.00

ISBN: 978-0-9557549-9-9